House Number 12
Block Number 3

Sana Balagamwala

Hidden Shelf Publishing House
P.O. Box 4168, McCall, ID 83638
www.hiddenshelfpublishinghouse.com

Copyright © 2021, Sana Balagamwala
Hidden Shelf Publishing House

Editor: Rachel Wickstrom

Cover art: Kristen Carrico

Interior layout: Kerstin Stokes

Library of Congress Control Number: 2021910044

Publisher's Cataloging in Publication Data

Names: Balagamwala, Sana, author.
Title: House number 12 , block number 3 / Sana Balagamwala.
Description: McCall, ID: Hidden Shelf Publishing House, 2021.
Identifiers: LCCN: 2021910044 | ISBN: 978-1-7354145-7-7 (paperback) | 978-1-7354145-8-4 (ebook)
Subjects: LCSH Family--Fiction. | Young women--Fiction. | Mental illness--Fiction. | Sexual abuse--Fiction. | Post-traumatic stress disorder--Fiction. | Pakistan--Fiction. | Karachi (Pakistan)--Fiction. | Civil war--Pakistan--Fiction. | Bildungsroman | BISAC FICTION / World Literature / Pakistan | FICTION / Own Voices | FICTION / Multiple Timelines | FICTION / Coming of Age | FICTION / Historical / General
Classification: LCC PS3602.A5934 H68 2021 | DDC 813.6--dc23

For my parents,
Farzana and Yusuf.

The grass is like me —
Its true nature revealed
When trodden under foot
But when drenched
Does it bear witness
To burning disgrace
Or blazing fury?

Kishwar Naheed

گھاس بھی مجھ جیسی ہے
پاؤں تلے بچھ کر ہی، زندگی کی ُمراد پاتی ہے
مگر بھیگ کر کس بات کی گَواہی بنتی ہے
شرمِساری کی آنچ کی
کہ جذبے کی حِدّت کی

کشور ناہید

1

**Karachi, Pakistan
December 1981**

The sound of the doorbell stirs those who slumber, but Zainab is already awake. She switches on the hallway light and hurries to the foyer, glancing for a moment at the walnut longcase clock that stands in the corner. The steel pendulum sways with resolve, and the minute hand staggers to twelve. It is five a.m.; too early for a guest to call, too early even for the vegetable seller who will come by at sunrise advertising bitter gourd so persistently that she'll buy some just to appease him.

It is five a.m.; revelers are stumbling home from a night out, the pious are returning from early morning prayers at the mosque, and those fortunate enough to be asleep are dreaming of those unspoken and unspeakable matters of the heart that confront us only in the night.

Zainab knows who is at the door, but she peeks through the peephole just to make sure. There has been an upswing in robberies of late. She unbolts the worn-out brass lock, and with a clang, my door creaks open. It is our gatekeeper. He adjusts his disheveled turban and greets Zainab with heavy eyelids. Behind him stands Apa, her frail form barely visible in the dim light of the overhanging pendant.

"Thank you for coming," Zainab says. Her voice is hoarse, her face a wrung-out rag. Apa steps past the jasmine topiaries into the foyer. Her silver hair is covered with a black muslin scarf; her feet are wrapped in brown sandals that crisscross her toes like bandages. She has come to see Nadia.

Nadia, who doesn't remember what day it is and who doesn't seem to care. Nadia who scribbles in notebooks, and cries when everyone is asleep. Nadia who sometimes forgets that her father just passed away.

We are still in mourning.

"I'm so sorry to bother you at this hour," Zainab continues. "She wouldn't stop crying. I didn't know what to do." Zainab smooths her kameez and tucks some stray wisps of hair behind her ear. Grays streak her bun, revealing months of forgotten hair appointments. A cool morning breeze wafts in through the open front door bringing with it the scent of jasmine as if to remind us, that still, there is hope.

"It's no bother," Apa says kindly. "Is she like she was the last time?"

Zainab nods and draws her gray scalloped shawl tight around her shoulders. A plain maxi flows out from under the shawl; the muted, unfussy attire of a woman mourning her husband. She shuts the door behind her and leads her guest upstairs toward the bedrooms. In the foyer and hallway, the curtains hang heavy, embroidered with brocade and sorrow. Melancholy has settled comfortably on the Persian carpets that languish across the floor.

"She hasn't come out of her room for three days," Zainab says. "Typical for her, so I just let her be. We've been taking her food and cajoling her into eating a little. When I woke up for Fajr prayers, she was crying incessantly, and trembling, like a child possessed. I think the jinn is back. I didn't know what to do, so I called you."

She pauses for a moment and sighs. "Apa, it is too much for me."

The dim light from the sconces illuminates the gallery of picture frames on the wall, relics from happier times. There is a photograph from long ago, but I remember the day well. Eid morning. Nadia is sitting on her father's lap, in a yellow dress of crinkled chiffon, her hair neatly brushed and fashioned into two fishtail braids, her smile missing the two front teeth. Haji Rahmat is laughing, the grooves that creased his brow in middle age are not yet visible.

"Did you give her any anxiety medication?" Apa asks.

"Half a pill to calm her nerves," Zainab says. "She is already on so many prescriptions. I don't want to give her any more."

"Perhaps the doctor should increase the dosage?" Apa wonders. "Your husband's death aggravated her condition, she may need a little more than before."

A low sob escapes Zainab's throat. "The medication he prescribed is for mentally ill patients," she whispers, as though worried that someone will hear. "My daughter is not mentally ill."

Apa glances at Zainab sympathetically and gives her hand a squeeze. "Did the nurse come yet?"

"No. Not yet. She will be here at eight a.m."

The door to the bedroom is slightly ajar. Zainab knocks softly and pushes it open. The curtains are drawn, and the room is dark except for the yellow glow of the night lamp that illuminates the bed in a fuzzy bubble of light.

Nadia is sitting up in bed, her back against the low wooden headboard, her head buried in her lap. Her hair is uncombed and matted. Even though it is not cold, she shivers under a thick woolen blanket that Zainab draped around her. At intervals, she exhales hollow, empty gasps.

Apa goes to her. She has seen this before. We have all seen this before.

"Salam beta," she says.

Nadia digs her thumbnail into her cuticles and picks at the raw skin. A tremor convulses through her body. Apa sits down next to her and takes her hand, squeezing it tight to stop it from trembling. She strokes her head gently. "It's alright," she says.

"You're okay."

The elderly woman retrieves an assortment of objects from her bag and lays them on the bedside table—a packet of herbs, a two-inch rectangular strip of paper, a black square cloth, and some string. On the strip of paper, she transcribes a prayer for wellness, in precise Arabic script. She folds it into a square, half-inch by half-inch. She wraps the paper with the cloth and secures it with string, as though wrapping a miniature gift. She gives the amulet to the young girl, who is still trembling. "Put it under your pillow," she says.

Nadia glances up. She has her mother's eyes, green with glints of gray. When Nadia was born and opened her eyes to the world for the first time, the nurses had marveled. Among a sea of babies with dark eyes, her eyes were one in a thousand. *She's won the genetic lottery;* the nurse had remarked. Prayers were said, and two goats had been sacrificed to protect her from nazr—evil eye. Now Nadia's eyes are vacuous, and her hair is thinning; clumps lay on her pillow as though someone comes and pulls it out in the night while she sleeps.

"I don't want to see him," Nadia says softly. She has run out of tears, but sorrow has not had its fill; there are dark caverns beneath her eyes, and her cheeks are sunken like caves.

I cannot bear to see her like this. A twenty-year-old needs to be vibrant, and delirious at the promise of life. She should not be like this, not like an old spinster–broken and bearing the burdens of the world.

"There is no one here," Zainab says to her daughter. "It's just me and Apa. You had a nightmare, again."

I don't know if Nadia hears her mother but her eyes dart around the room, like an injured rabbit hiding from a wolf.

"You're okay. You don't have to see anyone," Apa speaks softly.

To Zainab, she says, "bring some warm water. I'll make her some tea. It will help her anxiety."

Zainab withdraws from the room and returns with a mug

of warm water. Apa drops a packet of herbs into it and stirs vigorously. Some particles dissolve, the big bits and leaves dance about on the surface. "Here, take a sip," she says. Nadia drinks.

"Some more, beta, at least half," Apa prompts.

Zainab turns on the wall sconce. The yellow gleam divulges the disarray in Nadia's room; it has been a few weeks since it has been cleaned. She won't let anyone in to do it since her father passed away. The desk in the corner by the window is stacked with books and school coursework, overdue, forgotten. Behind the books, slightly visible, are scribbles on the wall. When she is alone, Nadia makes notes in notebooks and sometimes on the wall.

The light reveals the worry lines that dart across the young girl's forehead. She winces in discomfort as though it will betray her secrets and covers her face with the blanket. "It's too much for me," she says. "The light."

Zainab flicks the switch off and again we are left in the dark. Apa talks to Nadia and reads out prayers. An hour passes, and I see the angst that simmers in the young girl's eyes begin to subside. Perhaps it is prayer that soothes her, perhaps it's Apa's presence; Nadia closes her eyes and drifts into sleep.

Zainab and Apa talk in hushed voices while she sleeps. They discuss the possibility of the jinn possessing her body. Why else would she be this way, Zainab wonders? Why else would she waver between sanity and madness, break into anxious fits of fear and tears with no reason, refuse to leave her room, or meet with anyone?

I think it too, sometimes, that a jinn has taken over the girl. But I know things that Zainab doesn't, and her ignorance is a burden I must bear.

***

Daylight dissipates the early morning darkness, and the streets begin to come back to life. Neighbors out for a brisk morning walk to ward off cardiovascular disease, chaukidars perched outside gates on rattan stools drinking their morning tea, and Mrs. Khalid next door buying okra; they all pretend to go about their day and not to notice, but they see Apa leaving. They've seen her come and go before, and they know Apa visits us at House Number 12 on Block Number 3 because Nadia has gone mad.

2

It is a curious existence, that of a house. Boarders come and go, but I endure, through the ebb and flow of circumstance, unmoving and, some may say, unmoved. The deed of ownership placed in the iron safe in Zainab's bedroom summarizes my existence on a worn sheet of laminated paper. "Plot size of three thousand square yards, building size of one thousand square yards, owner(s): Haji and Zainab Rahmat, purchase date 1957."

Now, with Haji Rahmat's death, and discussions of selling, it appears as though I will be vacant once again.

A month ago, Junaid had brought up again, the idea of selling my grounds to builders who were encroaching into the neighborhood, and tearing up old houses to replace them with apartment buildings. Instead of continuing to live in an area that would soon be congested, he insisted the family move away to the quieter suburbs, away from the clamor of Karachi's city center. But like every other time Junaid broached this topic, Haji Rahmat turned him down this time too.

"If we move away," Junaid began, "there is a chance Nadia would get better." He paused and studied his father's face before continuing. "We've tried so much—medicine, therapy, prayer, it doesn't feel like anything is helping. She is getting worse, descending into madness."

Haji Rahmat would not hear it. "She isn't mad," he said. "If moving meant Nadia would be herself again, I would move in a heartbeat. But to uproot in the hope that she will be cured is a fool's errand."

Junaid tried to coax his father. "It's worth a try, isn't it Abbu? There is something wrong here, with this house."

I cringed at the blame appropriated on me. I knew it wasn't entirely true what Junaid said, but it wasn't entirely false, either. And so, I felt the bitter burden of responsibility. Perhaps some of it had been my fault after all?

Haji Rahmat disagreed with his son. For a moment he was deep in thought. Then his brow furrowed, his eyes betrayed stubborn resolute, and he shook his head.

"Listen to yourself speak," he said. "What could be wrong with a house? This place has been good to us. This house was my first home in this city, in this country! It was the place both you and Nadia were born. It gave me hope when I had none, and I am grateful for its blessings."

Junaid was silent. Haji Rahmat continued. "So, we uproot and move, and she is still the same. Then what?"

"I don't know. At least it won't be for lack of trying."

"Let it go, son," Haji Rahmat said. "I have enough on my mind. The day I leave my home will be the day you carry me out of here in my coffin."

A fortnight later, Haji Rahmat passed away in the middle of the night, and left behind his wife, two children, and a thousand *only ifs* and *what nows*. And so it was, that even in death, Haji Rahmat had his way.

3

Barrister Akhtar is seated in the formal drawing room. It has been fourteen days since Haji Rahmat's funeral. Zainab is in iddat, the customary waiting period for a widow, and prefers not to leave the house, so Junaid has requested the barrister come over to discuss matters of Haji Rahmat's will.

The sofas and tables have been pushed back toward the edge of the room to create space for prayer, and rugs are laid out over the black and white mosaic floor. Copies of the Quran are stacked neatly on the carved wooden end tables next to bowls of prayer beads, so that people who come to extend condolences can sit and say a prayer, offer a kind word, or share some news from the outside.

Nisar is in the kitchen preparing chai, and egg sandwiches. I think back to when he joined us quite accidentally, many years ago, a ruddy-faced boy of seven or so. He is eighteen now, or so he says, and we believe him, because his mother lost her memory so there is no one to verify what year he was born. He has long graduated from being the children's mischievous playmate to Zainab's house hand. Now he manages the kitchen and oversees the rest of the house staff. Haji Rahmat's death has been hard on him too, though he tries to be strong for the family's sake.

Nisar places four plates, Wedgwood with blue borders, on the tea trolley. He refolds the embroidered linen napkins, puts them on the bottom shelf, and straightens the silverware. He sets the ivory-colored teapot and matching teacups on the top shelf next to the plate of sandwiches, surveys the arrangement, and rolls the trolley toward the drawing room. Nisar has learned from Zainab the way of the household; the importance of keeping up a respectable appearance, no matter what the circumstances.

***

Upstairs in his bedroom, Junaid buttons his shirt, maneuvers his tie into a double knot, and glances at the wedding photograph of his parents that rests in a silver frame on the dresser. Haji Rahmat is laughing, and Zainab is smiling demurely behind her sheer veil. When Junaid laughs, his nose crinkles the same way as his father's. But there is not much to laugh about these days. Since his father passed, Junaid, at the age of twenty-four, has been given the sudden responsibility of running the factory and managing the business. He tries hard to be strong for his mother and sister, but I see him lie awake most nights, unable to sleep.

On his way to meet with the barrister, Junaid passes his sister's bedroom. The door is shut. He turns the door handle and frowns to find that it is locked.

"Nadia," he says and knocks on the door. "The barrister is here. We need to talk about Abbu's will."

A few minutes pass. He knocks again, tilts his head, and leans it against the door. There is no answer; no sound of rustling sheets or blankets, no shuffling of feet walking to the door, no sound of a key being turned in a lock.

"Come on, Nadia," he says. "Open up, please. It's hard for me to talk to you through this door."

Nadia does not open the door. She does not get up from her bed. She has a notebook on her lap and is writing something. Carefully, meticulously, she transcribes the same sentence over and over.

"There's rosemary, that's for remembrance; pray, love, remember; and there is pansies. That's for thoughts."

"Please, Nadia," Junaid calls through the heavy wooden door. "Just come out for ten minutes. I wouldn't bother you if it wasn't important."

I know Nadia can hear her brother.

She peers at the door, snaps her notebook shut, and tucks it under the mattress. She makes another tally mark on the wall on the side of the bed. She takes a sip of water to swallow a pill, closes her eyes, and covers her head with her blanket. Junaid waits five more minutes and knocks again. Then he gives up, shakes his head, and walks away.

***

In the drawing room, Zainab is seated across from the barrister. His briefcase lies open on the table between them.

Junaid greets the barrister. "I'm sorry my sister will not be joining us," he says.

Zainab's cheeks bloom a tinge of pink. "Poor Nadia is under the weather today. We can go on without her." Then, as though unsatisfied with her excuse, she adds, "It's the flu medication she took last night. It makes her so sleepy."

Annoyance flits over Junaid's face. It appears as though he wants to say something, but he purses his lips and holds back. He has gotten used to his mother making excuses for his sister.

A few months ago, some old friends of the family had come over for dinner. Nadia didn't come out of her room, not even to join the guests for dinner.

When the guests inquired about his sister, Junaid spoke up, but Zainab interrupted before he could finish his sentence.

"Oh, she's just very tired," she said quickly. "From all the studying lately. Finals, you know." She tilted her head and her nervous laugh lingered just a little too long. "She has been up all night studying for her exams and must have fallen asleep a few minutes before you arrived."

Our guests nodded with understanding. They had a daughter who went to the same university as Nadia, and I imagined they knew that Nadia had not been to class in a few months.

"Why do you make a thousand ridiculous excuses?" Junaid questioned his mother after the guests had left. "Just tell them the truth. That she is sick. And doesn't like to meet people."

Zainab, who was supervising the transfer of leftovers into boxes to be refrigerated, glared at her son. "Have you lost your senses?" she scolded and pressed the lid onto the plastic container with a click. "We can't say that. People always assume the worst. They are going to think she has some awful, incurable disease."

She handed Nisar a stack of boxes and continued. "Anyway, one of these days Nadia will be fine. But people will remember her as having some Godforsaken illness. It will be a blemish on her, forever. Remember what happened with Akbar?"

Akbar was Haji Rahmat's second cousin. As a child, he had suffered from seizures. His mother, in her worry, made a hue and cry about it, instead of keeping it to herself. The words that followed him through the rest of his life were these: he is a nice boy from a wealthy family, but since he was epileptic as a child, it affected his brain. Nobody was willing to give him their daughter's hand in marriage, not even poor families hopeful for their daughters to marry up.

Like all of us, Junaid heard Akbar's story several times, on several different occasions, with embellishments based on each narrator's preference. So now, with the barrister in the room, he knows to let it be, to let his mother make her excuses, and to let her think that people actually believe them.

Nisar pours out a cup of tea for the barrister. His hands shake a little. A few drops of tea splash out of the teacup. Embarrassed, he quickly wipes them up with the towel.

"How much sugar will you take, Sir?" he asks.

The barrister holds up two fingers and Nisar stirs brown crystals of sugar into the cup before he sets it on the table. The teaspoon clinks against the edge of the teacup in the silent room.

"Haji Rahmat was truly one of a kind," the barrister says and takes a sip of chai. "The community feels his passing greatly."

The olive jacquard curtains are pulled back and secured to the side with a cream-colored tassel. The sunlight from the window reflects off the barrister's gold-rimmed spectacles.

Junaid taps his fingers on the arm of his chair. "Thank you for your kind words, Barrister," he says. "I'll get straight to the point. We are already in the process of packing and we will move right after Ammi is finished with her waiting period. What we need your help with is getting the documentation in order, so we can sell the house as soon as possible."

Barrister Akhtar shuffles through the stack of papers in his lap. He takes out a handwritten sheet and hands it to Junaid.

"Mr. Junaid," he begins. "A few months ago, your father came into the office and requested we file this letter with his will. Have you seen it?"

Junaid reaches over to take the letter and assesses the paper. It is dated July 16th, 1981 and written in Haji Rahmat's handwriting. Zainab stares at her son. "What is it?" she prompts him. "Read it out loud for me."

Junaid scans the text and his face falls.

"Read it aloud, please," Zainab prods. Reluctantly, Junaid begins to read:

> *My dearest Zainab, my pride Junaid, and Nadia, the light of my life:*
>
> *If you are reading this, I am probably not among you anymore. It pains me to have left you alone, but I hope you will be there for each other through this trial."*

Junaid's voice breaks, and he pauses for a moment. The Barrister nods patiently.

I know we have talked much about this house; we have been through much together here. I know that Junaid wants to move, but my last request to you is to keep the house. Do not sell it. It brought me so much happiness. It was my first home in this new country, and it was the place both our children were born. I am happy that I lived out my days here, and I hope you will take care of our home and choose to stay here after I am no longer with you."

There is silence for a few minutes. Zainab's lower lip quivers. Her eyes are rimmed with tears, and she has shrunken into herself.

"I don't know what to say," Junaid utters, finally.

Zainab buries her face in her hands. Junaid gets up and goes over to console her. "Ammi, it's fine. Please don't cry." He squints at the barrister. "I'm not sure what to make of this."

The barrister purses his lips. A heavy silence has again descended in the room.

Then Zainab speaks, "I ... I don't want to move away from here, not now."

Junaid's eyebrows jump up. "Why? What is to be gained by staying here?"

"I just want to respect your father's wishes. Maybe it is too soon now."

"Ammi, every morning we wake up with the sound of some contractor bulldozing a house in the neighborhood. The air quality is terrible. The traffic is atrocious because of all the apartments they have built around us. And there's Nadia. Why should we insist on living here?"

"Beta, please."

Junaid kneels on the ground next to his mother and takes her hand in his. "Ammi, please. I respect Abbu's wishes, but he is no longer here."

"I know. That is why I can't leave. He is right; we have so many memories here. Soon, I will be gone too. You can move away then."

Junaid peers into her face as though searching for a reason to be convinced; finding none he says, "You're letting your emotions make decisions. This is ridiculous. We have outlived our time in this house. Think rationally. Please."

Zainab buries her face in her dupatta.

Junaid stands up. "What would Abbu have us do with the house? Dig graves and bury ourselves in it?"

"Junaid!" Zainab says, her voice raising an octave.

Junaid hands the letter to his mother. "Ammi, stay if you want. I'm moving away."

Zainab stares at her son, and back at the paper. "Barrister, what do you recommend?"

"Oh, Mrs. Rahmat. That is not for me to advise. It's a request from Haji Rahmat, may God rest his soul. It is not a legally binding document."

"Exactly," Junaid says. "It is not legal. It's a recommendation. Why does he expect us to stay here even when he is gone?"

"Junaid, please."

Junaid throws his head back and sighs in frustration. I wonder if he notices the slight discoloration on the right corner of the ceiling. The pipe in the second-floor bathroom has developed a leak, and the pooling water overhead has made its way through the cement and plaster.

Zainab collects herself quickly; she wipes her eyes with the edge of her dupatta and turns to the lawyer. "Barrister, please have some chai. It's getting cold."

Junaid walks toward the door. "I have another meeting I must get to Barrister," he says. "Thank you for coming, but there is nothing further to discuss unless you can convince Ammi there is no need to hold on to this property. Please excuse me."

As he disappears, Zainab apologizes fervently to the barrister about her son's outburst.

The burden of being despised and unwanted weighs tremendously upon me. It has been building for some years now, this quiet resentment of Junaid's, this notion that somehow, I am to blame for the tribulations that have befallen the family, this anger that Nadia's illness is somehow my fault, that I am cursed, and because they live here, they too have inherited the curse.

But it has not always been like this. Have they forgotten that once we were all deeply happy?

4

1957

It had been ten years since my previous owners had disappeared. Their gatekeeper had stayed on for a few months after they left, and his radio kept me updated on the goings-on in the city. Oh, the things I heard—of war, destruction, and horror; of people fleeing, of families breaking, and of homes being deserted—as allegiances were made and nationalities were picked following the Partition of 1947. But then, when the gatekeeper packed his belongings and hurriedly left one morning, I reluctantly became accustomed to spending my days alone and uninhabited. And so, except for the occasional company of the street cats, who found my empty spaces comforting, and the newspaper boy who sometimes tossed an evening tabloid in over the gate, I remained mostly undisturbed.

It was a Tuesday morning in November, and a thick marine layer had ventured far from the sea inland. The saline air wrapped itself wistfully around the balustrades of the front veranda, which were desperate for a new coat of paint.

First, I heard them: a motor engine coughing to a stop, crushed twigs and leaves protesting under the weight of heavy footsteps, and the grating sound of a key being forced into the padlock of the gate.

I wondered who it could be. Were my owners back? Maybe a replacement gatekeeper was finally here? Perhaps someone was breaking in. But a vagabond or a squatter mistaking the quiet grounds for a safe house would surely not have had the decency to use the gate—he would have leapt over the boundary wall, or rat-like, found his way through the hole in the crumbling northwest corner wall.

Then I saw them. A small group of people clustered around the wrought iron gate, combining all their efforts to coerce the padlock into submission. The gate creaked open on hinges that needed oiling, and a young man stepped inside, his entry announced by cigarette smoke and agarwood.

He must have been in his early twenties. He wore a well-tailored suit of powder blue and beige oxfords. He was clean-shaven and a Roman nose dissected his angular face with a pleasant symmetry. His eyebrows, thick and unruly, were the same color as his black karakul cap. He scanned the property and when his eyes finally rested on the front porch, he smiled and gazed at me with some semblance of gratitude and hope.

A young woman, no older than nineteen, stepped in behind him. She had striking green eyes; her hair was pulled back in a long braid, which swung over her left shoulder. A blue chador embroidered with yellow paisleys enveloped her. Another man dressed in a crisp white shirt and brown trousers followed the couple.

The man in the blue suit looked up at me, with dark eyes that brimmed with tears. His brow creased, and I wondered what he thought about. Then, he knelt down and kissed the ground still damp from last night's dew.

"Home at last," he said in a whisper that reverberated through the ground. "Home at last. Praise be to God. I am home at last."

I wondered who this man was and why he thought he was home. I was certain that I had never seen him before.

The woman with eyes like seafoam knelt next to this man and took his hand in hers.

"So, here we are," she said. "This will be home. How sweet the air smells."

A soft clear voice; like waves lapping against the seashore. She drew her chador around herself, smiled, and stood up carefully, holding her companion's hand.

The man in the brown trousers—a stout man with an impressive mustache, cleared his throat to get the couple's attention and then spoke. "Sir and Madam, please follow me."

He pointed out the gatekeeper's empty room by the gate, the rows of trees that trimmed the boundary walls; neem, jamun, and coconut palms, and led the couple down the paved driveway. The gardens to the right of the driveway needed reseeding, and mosquitoes were prospering in the waterlogged flowerbeds. The group did not pay much attention to the frightfully embarrassing gardens, but rather made their way to the front steps.

Upon reaching the marble steps, the man with the mustache pointed out the local yellow stone and the Burmese teak used in my construction. Then gleaming with appreciation, he added, "Look at these beautiful columns, in the design of an Italian villa."

I forgave the mustached man his design faux pas because he gestured with such gallantry towards the two neoclassical columns that framed my front veranda.

As they walked up the marble steps to the front door, I felt a twinge of embarrassment. The space that had once housed an elegant display of potted rose bushes was now a mess of broken terra cotta and dried twigs. The twelve-foot wooden windows on either side of the door were sun-bleached, and I noticed there seemed to be more cobwebs suspended from the louvered shutters today than usual. I hoped the exquisite detailing on my front door would be enough to distract them. The mustached man took his jangle of keys and tried two in the lock without success while the others glanced around. The gentleman in the blue suit did not seem disillusioned by my decrepit veranda, nor was he impressed by my front door. He appeared pensive, turning around periodically to survey the grounds, the gardens, and the driveway. Finally, the third key worked, and the door was unlocked.

"You first," the gentleman in the blue suit said to his companion with a smile. The young lady stepped in cautiously, glancing up at the crystal chandelier in the foyer, that despite the layer of dust still managed to glint in the sunlight. The man in the blue suit followed her in. He did not look up, but down, and his eyes lit up at the sight of the mosaic floor in the foyer.

"Zainab," he said. "The floor. It's like my grandfather's home in India."

He stood mesmerized by the pattern of interlocking diamonds in blue and mustard that dissected the circles on the floor. His eyes filled with tears and I mused about the home he spoke of. What did he leave behind, I wondered, and whom? Zainab, his companion, grasped his hand a little tighter and smiled at him.

"I wish your father could have seen this too Haji," she said.

The group walked through the drawing and dining rooms, which flanked either side of the foyer. They meandered through the first floor, through my kitchen and breakfast room, and when Zainab mused that the kitchen was small, her companion offered possibilities for renovation. Satisfied, they made their way to the spacious living room where Zainab peeked out of the windows, smiling approvingly at the garden outside.

"This door opens to the garden," the guide said proudly, as though he were responsible for the louvered french doors that connected the living room to the patio. Haji, the man in the blue suit, nodded in approval and glanced towards the staircase that extended upwards. Sunlight flooded in through the skylight in the second-floor ceiling, bathing both the staircase and the mustached guide who stood at its base in the mid-morning light.

"What's that door next to the staircase?" Haji asked pointing to a small door that blended into the wall.

"That is just a room used for storage," the man responded. He unlocked the door, and everyone peered into the dusty room. It was dark, except for the light that came in through the long windows along the rear wall.

"There is another garden behind the house!" Haji exclaimed,

noticing the back garden that was visible through the windows.

The guide bobbed his head in enthusiasm. Zainab glanced up at the landing towards skylight on the roof. "Can we go see what is upstairs?" she asked. The guide smiled and gestured to lead the group up the stairs. "What an unusual design," Zainab remarked, admiring the wrought iron banisters that seemed to grow organically out of the marble staircase. As she made her way up the staircase, she ran her fingers along the circular pieces of green onyx embedded in the iron banisters.

Upstairs, the visitors meandered through my spaces, their footprints stirring up the dust that till then had been allowed to accumulate undisturbed. Dreams hung suspended from cobwebs in the vaulted ceilings, and the bedrooms, curious to see who had awakened them from their slumber, opened their doors. A family of pigeons that had built a nest and settled comfortably into the wooden window frame of an open ventilation window snapped their beaks and squawked in disapproval to see the visitors.

"Needs quite a thorough cleaning, doesn't it, Haji?" Zainab said in between sneezes. "But how wonderful to finally have our own home."

And it was just like that on a winter's day in November 1957, that I began a new chapter of my life, with my new owners, Haji Rahmat and Zainab who had come from India to start a new life in the quiet city of Karachi. It had been ten years since Partition, so I imagined that the process to get a home must have been complicated. I learned from their conversation that when they first arrived from India they had taken up house with a large group of people in an abandoned flour factory, and then had lived like nomads with relatives and friends. Finally, enough money had come through, and they had been able to make the purchase price.

Henceforth, this was going to be home, and although it was kismet that brought us together, Haji Rahmat felt an immense debt of gratitude to me. In keeping with the spirit of jubilance and hope that characterized those early days, I was named *"Manzil-*

e-Azadi"—the destination of freedom. The words were carved painstakingly on a rectangular marble plaque, and an arabesque border of black flowers was added. The day the plaque was mounted, a prayer was held, a goat sacrificed, and food distributed to the poor. Zainab and Haji Rahmat watched in immense joy as the mason set the plaque into the cavity on the wall, filled in the edges with cement paste, and wiped the excess with a damp rag.

5

1961

Past the foyer, in the living room, there is a gallery of photo-graphs. Taken over the years, they punctuate the years and serve as record keepers: anniversaries and birthdays, and leisurely Sunday afternoons; moments that seemed inconsequential back then, but in retrospect provoke longing and nostalgia, as happy remembrances are wont to. There is one that is my favorite: a sizable black and white portrait that takes center stage on the wall.

Haji Rahmat and Zainab are seated on a tufted settee in the garden. Junaid, dressed in a plaid button-down shirt and suede trousers, has been placed between them. His face is scrubbed clean, his hair parted neatly to the side and the stubborn cowlick on his head smoothed down with gel. A packet of chewing gum peeks out from his balled fist; Junaid wouldn't sit still for the photo, so the photographer bribed him with a substantial amount of chocolate. Haji Rahmat and Zainab are smiling. They are young, and the frown lines that in later years became a permanent fixture on Haji Rahmat's forehead are not yet visible. Zainab is pregnant. The year is 1961.

The news of Zainab's pregnancy had amplified Haji Rahmat's happiness. After the birth of their first son, Zainab had suffered a miscarriage. That had been traumatic, but Zainab was young, and they were hopeful that they would conceive again. Junaid was a handsome and healthy boy. There was financial prosperity to be grateful for: the flour mill had prospered, and Haji Rahmat had recently purchased a yarn-weaving factory. Since the only thing a man could want more than a prosperous business was the prowess of a son to help him run it, many felt Haji Rahmat was a man favored by fortune.

I found Haji Rahmat to be a very unusual man. Every night, after dinner and Isha prayers, he would sit on his mat and pray for a daughter. "I thank you for the blessing that is my son," he would whisper in prostration, perhaps so as not to sound ungrateful, "but I ask you, oh Allah for the gift of a daughter." I found this pecular, that a man already blessed by a son, should want a daughter. Surely, he should be grateful and relieved; everyone else in the community certainly was, and here he was praying for a daughter when all good sense and advice dictated that he pray for more sons.

As Zainab neared her due date, a new house hand, Jameela, was hired to assist Zainab with chores. She was a stout, compact woman who took great pride in her 18-karat gold nose ring, which was a wedding gift from her husband. Jameela made it her business to know everything and correct any opinions she disagreed with.

The day Zainab gave birth, Haji Rahmat had meant to take her and Junaid to *The First Annual Flower Show* at the Intercontinental Hotel. Needless to say, it was not the most convenient day for birth. Zainab woke up complaining of pain, but of late she was always in pain, so she didn't pay it much attention. She picked out a shirt for her husband and argued with him for insisting on heavy cream with his tea, even though the cardiologist recommended against it. These tasks exhausted her, and as Haji Rahmat drank his tea (with heavy cream), she lay on the sofa, exhaling sharply with each breath.

"Oh, I think something's wrong ... the contractions, they are very close together."

Haji Rahmat immediately phoned the doctor.

"No, she does not have a fever," he said into the phone. "Yes, that's true—no, no bleeding. Oh, yes, certainly."

"Zainab," he said as he hung up the phone, "the doctor said we should head to the hospital. It's probably a false alarm because you're a month away from the due date, but she would like to check. I'll call your mother and ask her to meet us there if you like."

Haji Rahmat helped his wife up from the couch.

"Alright, I'll meet you in the front. I just need to freshen up," she said. "Get the car ready please." She inched toward the bathroom, pale as a wilted tuberose.

Zainab stood in the bathroom doubled over the sink. Her face was now swollen and flushed. She splashed cool water on it, patted it dry, and applied crème. She rummaged in the drawer for her kohl and applied it to her eyes, but her hand was unsteady and the line meandered. She sighed at her reflection, drew her dupatta around herself, and made her way to the front of the house. When she got to the foyer, she called out to her husband, and crumpled to the floor.

"I cannot. I ... I cannot." she started sobbing. "Something is happening."

Haji Rahmat rushed to his wife and knelt down next to her. He gripped her hand tight and put his other arm around her back to lift her off the floor.

"Hold on, hold on. We can make it to the hospital," he said and kissed her head. "You'll be okay."

"Jameela!" he called out, as he tried to steady his wife and help her up. "Jameela! Hurry, call for an ambulance! We need to take Zainab to the hospital."

The next few moments everything was a blur and amidst the confusion and the cries, I could scarcely believe what was happening. While Haji Rahmat held his wife in his arms, the doctor and Zainab's mother waited at the hospital, and Zainab gave birth in the foyer, eight feet from my front door.

For a few seconds, or perhaps it was minutes, there was no sound except for the sound of Zainab's labored breathing. The usual demeanor of calm Haji Rahmat generally wore on his face had melted to distress. Zainab's eyes were closed, beads of sweat trickled down her face.

"Zainab, look at me," he pleaded.

"It's out," she whispered, her eyes still closed.

"It's a girl!" he said and lifted the baby into his arms. His voice cracked with emotion.

"Ah. Let me hold her. Get me a blanket. Please."

"I can't leave you here."

Zainab's voice was fading. "I need a blanket," she said.

"The baby ... there is no sound. Can you get up?" Haji Rahmat's voice was low.

"No ..."

"Oh God ..."

" I ... I think, I can't feel anything anymore."

"Zainab, stay with me."

There was the pounding of footsteps, Jameela and Junaid came running into the foyer.

"Ammi!" Junaid screamed. "What happened to Ammi?"

"Junaid, she is alright. Please hurry, go to your room, and get a pillow and blanket, please."

Junaid stood there, shocked by the sight of his mother on the ground and his father in tears. In his four-year life, I don't think he had ever seen his father cry.

"Jameela, hurry, hurry!" Haji Rahmat pleaded. "Call the hospital, Zainab had ... Zainab is ... The baby is here. For the love of God, bring some water and some towels ... a blanket! The baby—"

Jameela knelt down next to Haji Rahmat and put Zainab's head on her lap. Haji Rahmat was hunched over Zainab, holding the silent baby in his arms.

"Go, sir. I am here. I have her. Go get a midwife, call an ambulance. Go Haji, sir, get a midwife!"

Haji Rahmat remained still, stone-cold and motionless as though his body had become an extension of the marble floor. Zainab lay on the floor, breathing deeply.

Then we heard a whimper, a barely audible murmur that grew into a cry. That most life-affirming sound soothed our very beings and spurred us into action. Junaid ran to his room to get a blanket and pillow. Haji Rahmat, jarred back to a more useful state of consciousness, made Jameela sit next to his wife, and he reluctantly put the baby in her arms.

"Stay here with them," he ordered. "I will go get a midwife." He hurried outside and called out to Javed, the neighbor's son who was playing cricket in the street.

"Javed, call your mother, tell her to come over. We've had an emergency in the house." With those words, he got into the car and sped away to get a midwife.

Junaid returned to the foyer with a pillow in hand and an oversized blanket trailing behind him. Jameela lifted Zainab's head gently and gestured to Junaid to place the pillow under it. She draped the blanket over Zainab's legs and torso, using one corner to cover the newborn that she cradled in her arm. Junaid sat quietly on the side; his eyes glued to his mother's face.

Zainab's eyes betrayed panic, but she struggled to keep her composure for her son's sake. "I'm okay, beta," she said to Junaid, who looked absolutely petrified. She took his hand and touched it to the baby's head gently. "Look, your baby sister is here."

At that moment, Javed's mother, Mrs. Khalid, came running in. Without a moment's hesitation, she knelt, lifted the baby, and pressed it against the warmth of its mother's skin. Jameela held Zainab's head in her lap, stroked her hair, and repeated prayers.

"Oh Allah, take me, take me, just spare the mother and child," Jameela said, "Spare them and take me! Take me and spare the baby. Spare Zainab, spare her."

"Shh, shhh," Mrs. Khalid said. "No one is dying. The baby will be okay. Breathe. Just breathe."

After a few minutes that had felt like several hours, Haji Rahmat returned with a midwife. She cut the cord and cleaned the baby. Soon we heard the sound of sirens, and an ambulance pulled up to the front gate. Two paramedics hoisted Zainab and the baby onto a stretcher and loaded them into the back. Haji Rahmat gave Junaid a quick hug before he jumped into the ambulance.

"Ammi is alright, son. Don't you worry. You can go over to play with Javed next door. I will call you soon." To Jameela he said. "Stay with him and make sure he eats something. I'll be in touch."

Jameela took Junaid into the house as the sirens screeched and the ambulance disappeared out of eyeshot. In the quiet moments that followed, I watched Jameela clean the floor where Zainab had given birth and I relived the events of the past hour a hundred times. The smell of blood, Dettol, and fear were stinging. Would the baby live? She would, right? We had heard her cry, after all. But what if she didn't?

It was six hours later, at four thirty in the afternoon that the phone rang.

Junaid was still at Mrs. Khalid's house, and Jameela had returned to oversee dinner preparations. Her anxiety had gotten the best of her, and being unable to focus, she batted about the kitchen with her tasbih in hand, intermittently bursting into loud strings of prayer. At the sound of the phone ring, she ran with uncharacteristic nimbleness and speed to answer it. It was Haji Rahmat, calling from the hospital. As Jameela listened, the stress melted from her face, and her smile widened with each passing second. I felt a rush of relief. It was good news for sure.

"Alhamdulillah, Praise be to God! Mubarak!" Jameela spoke excitedly the minute she could get a word in. "How is Zainab Baji?"

I waited eagerly for more details and imagined the joy Haji Rahmat probably felt at having his prayers answered. Jameela listened to Haji Rahmat on the other end, but unable to control herself, covered the phone mouthpiece, turned her head to the side, and called out to the cook, who had just walked in. "Aray Khansama! Mubarak! Baji had a baby girl!"

She spoke into the phone, "What is her name, sir? When will Baji be home, sir? Who does she look like, sir?"

A brief pause.

"Sorry, sir. Yes sir, I got too excited. Forgive me. Yes, I will bring the bags to the hospital. And of course, Junaid as well. Yes, right away, sir. Very good, sir."

I'm not sure what made Jameela happier, the news that the baby was safe, or the fact that she was the one to hear the news first and was entrusted with the responsibility of informing the others.

I wondered about the new baby. She was a miracle, and it was a blessing from God indeed that she had survived. I felt instant love for this new child, and I felt that our fates would be intertwined and connected for a long time. I learned that Haji Rahmat had named his daughter Nadia.

Jameela ran through the house gathering supplies and calling out orders.

"Khansama, get Zainab Baji's tonic and soup ready. Lal Khan call the driver. Have the car brought out up front. And go get Junaid from Mrs. Khalid's house. We need to go to the hospital."

The luggage, which included tonic, soup, and Zainab's clothes, was loaded into the trunk of the car. I was left alone, eager for news of Zainab and baby Nadia.

***

Zainab and the baby were still at the hospital recovering, but Haji Rahmat, Junaid, and Jameela returned later that evening. Haji Rahmat looked relieved, as if a weight had been lifted off his shoulders. Junaid looked tired; Jameela, victorious. Lal Khan and Khansama, who hadn't heard much news since Jameela had been

33

away at the hospital—were excited to offer congratulations and get details about the new baby. At the dinner table, as he served dinner, Khansama inquired:

"Sir, how are Zainab Baji and the baby?"

Haji Rahmat poured a glass of lassi for himself and his son. "She is perfect, Khansama, by the grace of God. I couldn't ask for anything more. And Zainab is well. She is a strong woman. The doctors are amazed she is recovering so well."

Unsatisfied with the amount of detail Haji Rahmat provided, Jameela spoke up, reveling in the power she had. She had been there during the birth and been the only member of the household help who had seen Nadia at the hospital, this gave her a feeling of status and authority that she intended to use to full capacity.

"Oh, what a scare she gave us, that little shahzadi," she said. "I thought for sure we were done for. In fact, I made a mannat to fast for three days if she survived!"

"That was very thoughtful, Jameela," Haji Rahmat said and took a generous helping of lamb curry.

"My bracelets, too," Jameela continued, "I pledged to give them to charity in the name of God if Zainab survived. They aren't worth much, but they are my mother's, and a pledge is a pledge."

"Jameela, that is generous." Haji Rahmat said. "But there is no need. Keep your mother's bangles. I will give charity in lieu of them."

"A pledge is a pledge! I'm going to go to the Mazaar on my day off to give thanks." Jameela said and ladled daal onto Junaid's plate.

"Who does she look like, sir?" Khansama asked as he placed a stack of steaming rotis on the dinner table.

Jameela was quick to answer. "She has Zainab Baji's green eyes, but she's dark-skinned, like her father." She paused for a moment to get a reaction, but getting none, continued. "Anyhow, she is beautiful. In fact, the midwife was quite taken aback by her beauty. She was practically glowing when she was born, like a pearl fresh from the sea."

Haji Rahmat smiled. "What do you think, Junaid? Can you tell who your sister looks like?"

"Like a baby." Junaid said, in between gulps of mango lassi. "She has a lot of hair."

Jameela added rice onto the boy's plate. "That's right. I've never seen such thick, beautiful hair. Come now. Eat faster," she said. "You don't want your baby sister to become bigger than you now, do you?"

Junaid poked at his daal and scrunched his nose. "Do I have to eat this?" he grumbled. "It has green seeds in it."

Haji Rahmat raised one eyebrow at his son and gave orders to Jameela regarding the after school schedule.

"Tomorrow, pick up Junaid from school and take him to Zainab's mother's. I will come there directly after work."

Jameela was fluffed up with authority. She took her position of being in charge while Zainab was away very seriously.

"Most certainly, sir. Not to worry."

For the next few weeks, it was quiet, since Zainab had been taken straight from the hospital to her mother's home. There she could recover from childbirth without the daily hassles of running the household. For the next forty days, sending for groceries, overseeing the kitchen, and keeping the house staff on their toes would not be her concern. Junaid would spend most of his day after school at his grandmother's house too. In the kitchen, the only activity was Khansama preparing sweets that would be sent out with Nadia's birth announcements. For days the kitchen smelled warm, of ghee, walnuts, and molasses. Haji Rahmat ordered silver dishes, engraved with Nadia's name and date of birth. These were filled with walnut halwa, packaged with transparent plastic wrap and silver ribbons, and loaded into boxes for immediate delivery to neighbors and family members.

6

It has been twenty-one days since Haji Rahmat's funeral. The throngs of people coming to extend condolences have died down, as I expected. How much can outsiders mourn, after all? One must move on. Still, some days family members and friends trickle in to offer a kind word and comfort. Today, the gatekeeper announces that Nadia's friends are here.

"How are you feeling, Aunty Zainab?" Mariam says. She comes up the front steps to the veranda and gives Zainab a kiss on the cheek. Her family lives two streets away and Mariam and Nadia have been friends since they were five.

"Is Nadia here? We brought some food for her."

Another friend from school, Yumna, has come along, too. Both girls are still in their grey and white school uniforms, the creases on their clothes telling of a long, tiring day.

"Come in my dears," Zainab says. "It's always so lovely to see you. Yes, Nadia is in her room. Go on ahead." She closes the door behind them. "Hope you can convince her to eat, maybe cheer her up a little," she adds wistfully.

The door to Nadia's room is shut. Mariam turns the door handle and finding it locked, knocks loudly.

"Nadia, open up."

"We brought sandwiches. Come eat with us, we are starving."

They wait a few minutes in silence.

"Come out, we have to tell you about Yumna and her latest love affair."

"You know we aren't leaving till you come out."

Nadia opens her bedroom door. A pale-yellow shirt hangs on her shoulders as though on a bent wire hanger. She stands in the doorway, reluctant.

"God, you look malnourished," Mariam says. The girls envelop Nadia in a hug and drag her out to the living room.

"We really miss you," Yumna says. She sets the paper bags on the coffee table and settles cross-legged on the sofa next to Nadia. Mariam opens the box of sandwiches, sprinkles chili powder on the french fries, and passes them around.

"So, we get out of college, and guess who is waiting around the corner with flowers today in his big jeep?" Mariam begins.

Yumna blushes.

Nadia forces herself to speak. "Another one of your admirers?" She asks and eyes Yumna.

"Yes, obviously," Mariam licks the chili off her fingers. "You won't guess who it is this time."

Nadia reaches for the woolen blanket on the sofa armrest and wraps it around herself.

"Well, don't just sit there Nadia, ask me who it was!"

"Okay, who was it?"

"You're going to die!"

"Okay ..."

"You won't believe it!"

"Just tell me?"

"The chief minister's son," Mariam squeals in delight. "The boys just can't stay away from this girl."

Yumna turns even redder. "You make me sound like I'm awful for leading them on."

Mariam raises one eyebrow at her. "You do lead them on, though."

"No, I'm just friendly, they misunderstand."

"Right."

Yumna rolls her eyes. "Well, this time it feels different. He is so genuine. I think I may love him." She takes a big bite of the club sandwich, and a blob of mayonnaise plops on her lap. "Oh, great," she says. "Pass me a napkin."

Nadia hands her a box of tissues. "You're just in love with the idea of being admired," she says. "And maybe with his car."

Mariam howls in laughter.

"We miss you, Nadia. Come back to college, enough of this hibernating in your room. Please. We need you there to drum some sense into Yumna. She has still been flirting with that other boy. She collects boyfriends like we used to collect Barbie dolls."

Nadia almost smiles.

"Eat some fries," Yumna says, and holds the box out for Nadia. Nadia waves it away.

Yumna pops two crisp french fries in her mouth. "Oh, too much chili," she says and smacks her lips together.

Mariam continues. "He wanted to take her out for ice cream after college, but we were coming to see you, so Yumna had to refuse. The poor boy was so disappointed, he even offered to drive us both here."

"You didn't let him, did you?" Nadia says.

"Obviously not! We remember how your ammi was that time when Ali dropped us at your house."

Nadia smiles wryly at the memory. "I remember. She was so furious."

Every time Nadia smiles, I hope that maybe this is the moment it all turns around, maybe now she is healed, and maybe now she will be herself again.

Mariam laughs and feigns mock seriousness. "What will people say?" she teases. "That Haji Rahmat's daughter and her friends are roaming the city with boys?"

Nadia's smile has disappeared, and her eyes are dull again. They betray some semblance of sorrow, a wistful longing.

"Your sandwich is getting cold, Nadia. You haven't taken a single bite," Mariam says. "Eat something. You know I'm not beyond prying open your mouth and force-feeding you."

Nadia pretends to take a bite of her sandwich, probably so her friends will stop bothering her. "So, what are you going to do about him?" she asks.

Yumna flicks her thick brown hair over her shoulder. "I don't know," she says.

"He has quite a reputation," Mariam says. "Stay away."

Yumna pouts. "You say that about every boy who likes me." She gets up from the sofa. "I'm going to get something to drink," she says and walks towards the kitchen.

Nadia and Mariam sit in silence on the sofas. For a few minutes, the only sound is that of rustling paper bags and the crunching of almost burnt french fries.

"We ran into your ex-fiancé yesterday," Mariam says softly to Nadia. "He was asking about you."

Nadia sets her uneaten sandwich on the table and wraps the blanket tighter around her.

"I don't want to talk about it." Suddenly her face droops, she looks tired.

Mariam reaches over and gives Nadia's hand a squeeze. "Sorry, I didn't mean to bring that up. Forget I said anything."

Nadia hugs her legs into her chest and rests her chin on her knees.

"Come on, at least finish your sandwich," Mariam says.

Yumna comes back with a tray of drinks, a Pakola and two Mirindas. It is quiet in the living room and Yumna raises her eyebrows at Mariam in query. Mariam shakes her head, no.

"I really need to sleep now," Nadia says and gets up. "I'll see you later, okay? Thanks for coming."

Yumna and Mariam look crestfallen, their mission a failure.
"You sure?"
Nadia nods and disappears into her room.

7

1964

Nadia started collecting things when she turned three years old. At first, it was only stones, but then she moved on to living things: flowers and earthworms.

The household was very encouraging of Nadia's pursuits. Jameela feigned delight when Nadia presented her with three smooth pebbles. Junaid was actually sort of proud when Nadia told him how she saved an earthworm from death by a sparrow. Mostly alone, except for occasional company from Junaid, Nadia explored the gardens and came home with curious mementos. However, after finding three earthworms squirming on the kitchen counter one morning, Zainab laid down the law.

"Nadia, flowers are acceptable, rocks are fine, but there will be no earthworms in the house."

Nadia's face deflated like a balloon.

"What about butterflies, Ammi? Can there be butterflies in the house?"

Zainab answered instantly, stirring turmeric and honey into a mug of milk. "Sure, if you can catch one. They can live in the house."

Nadia listened with disbelief, and so overjoyed was she with her mother's permission that she enlisted help and began her mission to capture butterflies. Haji Rahmat, who was delighted by anything Nadia did, spent many hours researching the appropriate ways to catch butterflies without harming the food chain. Junaid helped her fashion a large net from mesh and the crocheting ring they found in the cupboard of old things. All afternoon, Nadia scampered around the gardens, waving her net in the air like a shaman on fire, and even in the evenings when she accompanied her father on his evening walk, she kept it by her side, just in case. But butterflies were hard to come by, and at the end of the week, with zero butterflies in her private collection, Nadia was near tears.

Zainab tried to console her daughter.

"It's expected my love. Butterflies are not meant to be in nets, they are meant to be free!" So, she brought out colored paper, lime green, lilac, and fuchsia and showed Nadia how to make origami butterflies. They hung the paper butterflies from the wooden posts on Nadia's bed, and as Nadia lay in her bed that night, Zainab told her the story of Psyche and Eros, and the legend that butterflies were souls of people who had left Earth.

Haji Rahmat came home the next day with two small boxes of larvae, a curious cylindrical cage made of net, and a sense of accomplishment.

"Why have paper butterflies, when you can have the real ones?" he announced as he handed the larvae to Nadia.

"Careful now, my dear," he said to his daughter, whose face had begun to beam like a full moon. "Place the larvae in the net and feed them well. Very soon, you will have your own plain tiger butterflies."

This is the way he was with her, always finding ways to give her what she desired. The next several weeks were spent in careful observation of larvae, feeding them and misting the cage to create a tolerable habitat for growth. Nadia and Zainab spent several afternoons in the library poring over Encyclopedia Britannica to make sure conditions were just right for metamorphosis, and every morning Junaid helped her pick the juiciest leaves from the garden to feed the caterpillars.

One morning Nadia awoke to find the chrysalises had unfolded into adult butterflies that flitted about in the net cage, flirting with their newly discovered ability to fly. She unzipped the net cover and set them free. The sun streamed through chinks in the curtains and Nadia watched her babies flicker about on rays of sunshine.

She called out to her mother and to Junaid who came into the living room to be greeted by seven fully-grown plain tigers ready for flight.

"Oh, my goodness! What happened here?" Zainab was bewildered. "How on earth did they escape?"

Nadia's face radiated pride. "Oh, they were ready to fly. I let them out." And then seeing the frown on her mother's face, she immediately realized she had made an error and tried to remedy the situation.

"You, you said butterflies don't belong in nets, Ammi, you said they should be free ... Oh? Did I make a mistake, Ammi? Are you angry?"

If Zainab was angry, she couldn't have stayed that way for long. For what we were confronted with was indeed spectacular. It was as though we were still asleep, dreaming, in a tropical wonderland the likes of which I had seen in the book, *Photographs from the Amazon,* where it was the most ordinary thing to have a butterfly float out of the irises in a painting on the wall, and see several others pause on the armrest of a wing chair.

For a few moments, there was silence, and we took it all in. Then Zainab smiled.

"Nevertheless, my love," she remarked. "We must let them out of the house."

That is what the rest of the household awoke to that morning: Zainab running around the living room opening windows to let the plain tigers out while Nadia, in her nightgown, danced amidst flickers of yellow-speckled brown wings.

Years later, I would often recall this day, when the only thing we had to worry about was how to get butterflies out of the house.

8

It is early morning, and a month has passed since Haji Rahmat's funeral. The gatekeeper is sitting on the worn plastic stool outside his room fiddling with the radio. A stream of static issues forth as he pushes buttons and turns knobs. He calls to Nisar, who is still inside the quarters. "Come here. Fix this darned thing for me!" he croaks. "Put your education to some good use."

Nisar has been awake for several hours but is lying in his charpoy deep in thought. He sits and glances at the small alarm clock at the corner. It is six thirty a.m. He cracks his back, gets out of bed, and puts on his kurta. He has to begin his chores soon.

"It's time for a new radio," Nisar says, peeking his head out of the quarters. "I've tried fixing it before, it's no use. This radio is gone, much like your youth!"

The gatekeeper laughs in spite of himself. He pours himself a cup of tea from the saucepan that is bubbling on the small floor stove.

A quiet stillness abounds. On a normal day, Haji Rahmat would have been awake, and the sound of rustling newspaper and brewing coffee would fill the kitchen. Zainab would have finished her tea and moved on to directing Nisar and Jameela with the day's tasks. But today Zainab is still in bed, the covers drawn over her head. She didn't sleep much last night, drifting into slumber only at four a.m., after the sleeping pill took effect.

Nadia is awake in her room. She has already showered and changed out of her pajamas. I am surprised and wonder what she is planning to do. She tiptoes to her bedroom door, unlocks it, and peers out. It is quiet outside—there is no whirring of the orange juicer from the kitchen, no swish of the jhapat as Nisar cleans the window netting, no sound of the morning news update from the living room TV. Satisfied that no one is awake, Nadia steps outside her room and softly shuts the door. She creeps cautiously towards what used to be her father's favorite room.

The library sits in quiet disarray. The light coming in through the windows highlights the shelves, half of which have been emptied of books. Cardboard boxes are stacked by the wall, and in the corner, by the antique wooden desk; Haji Rahmat's reading chair is empty. The auburn leather cracked with use, the water ring on the armrest where Haji Rahmat rested his teacup, the extra cushion to support his back, all are the same as when he used to be around. Nadia stares at the chair for a few minutes. Then she unbolts the wooden french doors that lead to the garden, and steps outside.

The roses are turning brown at the edges, and patches of dry grass have sprouted up. The leaves of the coconut palms droop, as though in mourning. The pink flowers of the overgrown oleander peek over the boundary wall. Nadia walks along the outer perimeter of the garden under the shade of the trees: neem, coconut, and jamun. A little tree stump marks the end of the garden and the beginning of a dry rectangular patch that runs almost ten yards in length. Here, many years ago Haji Rahmat, had a patch of land cleared to make a mini cricket pitch. Over the years the little tree stump became a scoreboard, where hopscotch wins, and wickets in games of cricket were recorded. While her father trained them on the cricket pitch, Junaid and Nadia would, in turn, keep track of runs and wickets on the stump. Now, with all its markings and grooves, the tree stump resembles an owl seated on the ground, its face covered with its wings. Nadia sits down on the stump and runs her fingers over the grooves and markings.

In the servant quarters, Nisar finishes his tea and begins his customary morning round of the grounds. He spots Nadia sitting on the owl tree stump at the far end of the garden. "Salam Baji," he calls out. "You're awake early today."

Nadia appears disconcerted and peeks up. "Oh, it's you," she says, seeming relieved to see Nisar. "I got scared. Why are you awake so early?"

"I always wake up at this time," he says and walks toward her. "Shall I make you breakfast?"

"I couldn't sleep," she says. She continues, sharing more than is characteristic of her these days. "I had a dream about Abbu. He was in the library, and then he came outside to the garden to read his newspaper. It was so real, that when I woke up, I had forgotten he was gone."

He studies her for a moment, sitting on the tree stump.

"Shall I clean your room now?" he asks.

"No. Not yet," she says, too quickly. "First make me some chai, please."

"Of course. But please don't forget to let me clean your room. Your mother has said I must clean it today. It hasn't been cleaned for ten days."

Nadia looks uncomfortable. She gets up and walks slowly behind Nisar, and they both make their way toward the kitchen. The morning is warming up already, and Nadia's wet hair is beginning to dry. Soon Zainab will wake up, and I know she will be happy to hear that Nadia ventured outside today without any prompting. In the wake of her husband's death, and her daughter's deterioration, these little things make Zainab hopeful and keep her going.

The storage shed that marks one end of the cricket pitch is bolted with chains and a hefty iron padlock. A crow is pecking on the decomposing carcass of a rat that lies outside the shed door. Nadia stops, jarred by the sight. Her shoulders tense, her face stiffens. She turns around abruptly, and runs back, through the garden, and through the library door that has been left ajar. Flushed and out of breath, she escapes to her room, shuts the door, and locks it. She sits down with her back against the door, in the darkness of her room, and closes her eyes.

In the kitchen, Nisar pours the chai into a cup and sets it on the dining table with Nadia's breakfast: one roti and a little smidgen of honey and cream. But Nadia is nowhere to be seen. A few minutes later, it is obvious she is not coming, so he takes her breakfast to her room. He knocks but there is no answer. He looks disappointed—perhaps because he missed the window of opportunity to clean her room, or perhaps because he too, like me, had felt relief and optimism to see Nadia outside her room. He sets the tea on the TV tray outside her door, knocks once more, and leaves.

9

1964

Zainab always maintained that a jinn lived in the trees in the rear garden, in fact, she insisted that the reason the garden was always in bloom was because of the jinn. Her suspicion was aroused, in 1964, when the first strings of renovations were planned.

Haji Rahmat didn't believe her. *The jinn only bother those who believe in them*, he repeated categorically. Zainab disagreed with her husband. She insisted the kids stay away from the back garden, but they never listened; and she would launch into a litany of scolding if the children played in the trees at sunset, which is when the jinn were believed to be most active.

The property that I sit on boasts two gardens. One flanks the gravel driveway and is visible upon entering the property. The second, the rear garden, the one always in bloom, lies behind my main structure. To get there you'd have to pass the gravel driveway and go around the side; past the flowerbeds, past the gate that leads to the servant quarters and bathrooms, past the deep wash basins where the dhobi washes the clothes, past the cricket pitch, and then turn right. There, right behind my structure, it lies like a hidden oasis.

This garden was Haji Rahmat's favorite spot. Here, the roses and chambeli, champa and carnations, bloomed year-round. The gardener received credit, but I know he did not deserve it. No matter the gardener, no matter the weather, when the rest of the gardens and flowerbeds shriveled up and turned brown, this little garden always blossomed. It was as though another god reigned here, and bestowed favor upon us in the form of foliage.

It irked Haji Rahmat that there was no access to this garden from my main structure. A small back room with a meager window was all that looked into the garden. So, he planned a renovation to convert the storage room into a library for himself, and to have the wall in the rear opened up and replaced with generous glass doors, so that when he drank his morning tea, he could enjoy the view. Since this renovation would render the room unsuitable for storage, a replacement room was to be constructed as well, on the outside towards the back of the property.

It was a simple project. Two laborers were hired, and work began immediately. A few days later as they broke through the first layer of plaster, the laborers were surprised to find the outline of a preexisting doorway that had been filled with bricks, covered with cement, and painted.

The older laborer commented first.

"Look. There was a door here before. Someone boarded it up."

The younger one grumbled, "first they board up a wall, then they want to open it up."

"What does it matter to you? You're getting paid."

"We'll probably be back next year to close it up again!"

"If that's what they want, that's what we'll do!"

He chipped at it some more, and a layer of paint cracked and crumbled away.

They continued hammering and finally, the bricks began to give way. Specks of plaster, dried paint, and asbestos flitted on the rays of sunlight that poured in through the openings in the wall. A light breeze was blowing outside. The air was suddenly fragrant; an intoxicating musk came in through the chinks in the wall and filled the air. The workers finished up the day's work late in the afternoon and went home.

The next morning the workers didn't show. Later in the day, the younger one came to speak to Haji Rahmat on his partner's behalf.

"Sir," he said, "my brother has taken very ill."

Haji Rahmat set his newspaper down and pursed his lips in annoyance. "What is the matter with him? When is he expected back? We can't be expected to live with a hole in the back of the house, now can we?"

"Sir, he didn't sleep all night, due to chills."

"So, arrange for some medication. Tell him to take some Paracetamol and come back to work in a day."

"It is a strange fever, sir. His eyes are wild and bloodshot." Lowering his voice, he added, after a moment's hesitation, "Mother says he has been affected by jinn."

Haji Rahmat threw his hands up in the air.

"You fool. You're going to pretend he's been taken over by a jinn to get out of a job? Be off with you. I'll find someone else to do the work. It is three days of work, and you both can't even manage that!"

The laborer left in embarrassment and Lal Khan updated Khansama, who reported it to Jameela. Haji Rahmat did not mention this episode to his wife. However, the breakfast dishes had scarcely been put away when the possibility of jinn hovering in the rear garden reached Zainab through Jameela. Zainab, knowing that her husband did not believe in this stuff, decided to do her own investigation and called an old friend of her mother's, a lady named Apa, who lived by herself and spent her time in prayer and contemplation.

Apa came and surveyed the property. She walked the rooms, and the servants' quarters outside; she sat for an hour outside in the garden. The result was a confirmation of Zainab's suspicions. Apa said that though one can never be sure, she did feel a heavy presence of some sort in the back of the house, especially the back garden, by the fruit trees. There was nothing that could be done, she said, but recommended a prayer for safety.

***

That evening, as Zainab and Haji Rahmat dressed for dinner, Zainab shared her findings with her husband.

"I called Apa to survey the house," she began. She sat on her dressing table in her sari blouse and petticoat, rummaging through the drawer. Her hair was lifted in an elegant bun.

"I see." Haji Rahmat avoided his wife's gaze as though he knew where this was going. "What shall I wear tonight?"

"I've had your blue shirt pressed. It's hanging in the closet," she answered. "So, I was worried about what happened with the construction worker—"

"He probably found a better-paying job elsewhere."

Zainab scooped out a dab of face cream in the palm of her hand and pressed it on her cheeks. While waiting for her skin to absorb it, she patted shadow on her eyelids, mauve and gold. Next, she applied her black eyeliner carefully, in the waterline, and on the eyelid, making a perfect winged tip.

"You should've told me about this, Haji."

"I didn't want to worry you with nonsense, my dear."

"Do you think the safety of our children is nonsense?"

Haji Rahmat shook his head and buttoned up his shirt. He opened the drawer in the dresser and perused the neatly laid rows of cufflinks. He picked up an enamel pair. "You like these?" he asked.

Zainab glanced over briefly. "No, wear the silver ones," she said. "Anyway, Apa was kind enough to walk through the whole house. She said the land feels heavy in the back, and that there might be a jinn in the trees."

"Of course she did."

"Perhaps the renovation so close to the back garden stirred

51

something up. In the jinn, I mean."

"Okay," he said. He fastened the silver cufflinks and tapped a bit of agarwood on his wrist. The scent of musk and wood warmed the room.

Zainab tucked a stray hair back into her coiffed bun. "Well," she prompted, "what do you think?"

"You look lovely, as always."

Zainab raised one eyebrow at her husband.

He sighed before continuing. "Fine, fine. Well, if you really want my opinion ... I don't believe it Zainab. It sounds ridiculous."

"I'm worried though. The children play there all the time. What if there is a jinn there?"

"Where is the qawwali tonight?" Haji Rahmat asked.

"Hotel Metropole," Zainab said. "Stop changing the subject."

"I'm not changing subjects." He checked his wristwatch and added, "We are going to be late."

Zainab wrapped her sari around her waist and pinned up three perfect pleats. "I'm almost ready." She drew the shaded fabric, pink and mauve, one more time around her front and slung it off her left shoulder.

"Okay, so say there is a jinn," Haji Rahmat asked her. "What does Apa recommend we do about it?"

Zainab checked her reflection in the mirror.

"Nothing," she said. "That's precisely the problem. We can't do anything. It was probably living here before we moved in. We just have to leave it alone."

"What you're saying is, we have a jinn living in the tree in our garden and all we can do is peacefully coexist with it," Haji Rahmat said, putting on his suit jacket.

"Well. I mean it sounds silly when you say it that way."

Haji Rahmat glanced again at his watch. "It sounds silly whichever way you say it. Are you ready?"

"Yes. Here, please fasten the clasp for me." She handed a pearl string to her husband and continued. "Maybe we need to build a wall or a gate of some sort. I don't want the children going back there."

"If the jinn wants to possess them, it will leap over the wall or gate to do so."

"Okay, then maybe we should move houses? Just to be safe. Why put all this money into renovation if there is suspicion of a jinn."

"That is an extremely exaggerated response! There is no proof of a jinn." He fastened the clasp at the nape of his wife's neck and continued. "Why would I leave my home to escape a possible belligerent jinn in a tree? It's not so easy to find another house. And for all we know; it may decide to move with us!" Haji Rahmat glanced again at his watch. "Come on, it's already half-past eight."

Zainab tossed a lipstick into the gold mesh evening bag that sat on the dresser and slung it over her shoulder.

"I'll have the car brought out front," Haji Rahmat said, and he slipped the tickets for the show into his coat pocket. "Check on the children, I'll see you outside." He glanced at her and added, "Zainab, don't worry please."

But Zainab still worried, and Haji Rahmat remained determined to build his library with a view of the garden. He had heard news that his father's ancestral home in India had been burned during a riot. It had devastated him. The rioters set fire to every room. The bathtubs had been filled with water and the books from his father's library dumped in them. That had been his impetus to complete his new library here, and he resolved to see it through.

So, Haji Rahmat recruited new laborers to continue his project. Once the doorway was cleared out, they knocked out the second-story rooms above it to add height to the ceilings and installed teak shelves that stretched from the mosaic floor to the ceilings. The scent of sawdust and furniture polish was suspended in the air as the shelves were fitted and stained. The broad shelves left no space for windows, so skylights had to be installed in the ceiling. Three sizable rectangular cavities in the ceiling were fitted with glass to allow in light. For access to the garden, two double doors were installed, wooden louvered doors that could be opened up completely. The storage shed outside was completed too, a bland room with an area of about 25 square meters. The room did not suit my aesthetic but fortunately was shielded from view by the kitchen and thus not visible from the front elevation. The entire renovation took six months. Except for the initial suspicious episode, everything went relatively smoothly, and as the construction wrapped up, and the dust dissipated, so did the anxiousness I had felt earlier.

Slowly the library was populated. Rumi, Ghalib, Iqbal and Austen, Dickens, Eliot, Tolstoy, and Hemingway filled the shelves. It was a glorious space and I felt satiated by the new additions. Friday evenings were my favorite time of the week. After Zuhr prayers, lunch and afternoon siesta, the family would sit in the library, where the children played board games, sometimes running into the garden to play hopscotch while Haji Rahmat drank his evening tea, and Zainab worked crossword puzzles in the evening newspaper.

It was one such evening, when Haji Rahmat was more contemplative than usual, that the conversation turned to the days in India.

Haji Rahmat rested his head back in his armchair and sighed. "It's been almost a decade since we moved to this house. How time passes, Zainab."

Zainab smiled. "Truly—I wonder how things would be if we had never left."

"We'd probably be dead," he answered, and then realizing his children were present, looked sheepish. Zainab glared at him.

Nadia, three-years-old, glanced up worried and curious. "Why would we be dead?"

"Abbu doesn't mean that," Zainab interjected and turned to the game of Ludo the children were setting up.

Junaid interjected. "He means dead, like so tired that you feel dead."

Nadia opened her mouth undoubtedly to question when Zainab spoke up. "Nadia, do you want blue or yellow? Junaid has picked red."

"I want light blue, please."

"They don't make light blue, just go for blue please. Let's start."

"Fine, I get to roll first."

Junaid protested, "She always goes first."

Haji Rahmat had the final word. "You're almost eight. Be a big boy now. Let your little sister go first."

Nadia squealed with joy and began to shake the dice with the intensity of one victorious; one used to getting her way.

As they played Ludo, Haji Rahmat and Zainab reminisced about a time that now seemed far away. When the Malhotras abandoned me in 1947, the riots in Karachi hadn't seemed that bad. I heard things on the gatekeeper's radio, but when he abandoned me, too, I had been left in the dark. But the horrors they spoke of! Zainab was still unmarried, a young girl of nine when she left India. She remembered her mother telling her and her baby sister to leave their toys for now, as they buried their gold and trinkets in earthenware pots in the ground, thinking when things settled, they would come back for them. She remembered sleeping (or lying awake really), on the roof that night before they left, armed with hot oil and chili powder, just in case. She recounted leaving home in the early morning before sunrise, before the rioters came running, before the predawn sky was set ablaze by torches that would set buildings on fire.

Haji Rahmat remembered his father forcing him to leave alone in the night on a one-way flight on Orient Airways from Bombay to Karachi. The rest would follow, his father told him, but as tickets were scarce it was important to take one when it became available. He recalled how he left reluctantly, a fifteen-year-old armed with nothing but hope and an allegiance to a new nation-state. How the air that night was tense, with the passengers expecting at every instance that the plane would be shot at or grounded, and how even the engines sighed in relief when the captain announced five hours later that they had crossed the Indian-Pakistani border. And how, when the plane finally touched ground it was seen as nothing short of a miracle and the passengers erupted in a round of applause and cheers punctuated by cries of, "home at last, home at last, praise be to God, we are home at last."

I wondered what else they remembered. But more than that, I wondered what they were trying to forget.

Haji Rahmat, particularly nostalgic, turned to his daughter who was now sour-faced because she was losing.

"Nadia, beta, do you know where I lived when we first came here, before we came to this house?"

The three-year-old gazed up and answered. "Yes, I know. I know. You lived in a flour factory with your cousins and when you came out no one could recognize you because you looked like a white man." Junaid and Zainab laughed at Nadia's retelling, because things were good now, and in retrospect these things are funny. Then I remembered what the poet Gibran had said about joy and sorrow, how they were inseparable, and always came together. *How when one sat alone with you at your board, to always remember that the other was asleep upon your bed.*

10

1965

The year had seemed to start well, with the hope of martial law being lifted and Fatima Jinnah, the Quaid-e-Azam's sister, running for presidential elections. Although the big cities from Dhaka to Karachi all rallied behind her, she lost the elections and Ayub Khan transitioned from being a military dictator to elected President. He had scarcely begun his presidential term when the skirmishes on our borders with India intensified and developed into a horrific war. We were shaken to our core: the cities near the border as well as those that were insulated felt the tremors of the earth as the tanks rolled over, and the rattling of walls as bombs descended. We blacked out our windows, kept lights dim at nights, and remained ready to retreat to underground bomb shelters at a moment's notice.

But war had united us, and a wave of patriotism swept over our country making us believe that we were invincible. Patriotic songs poured out of the radio, inspiring us and bolstering our self-confidence. I especially loved hearing Madam Noor Jahan sing; the beauty and emotion in her voice were unparalleled. Our armies were mismatched in numbers; India having a significantly larger force, but our soldiers performed so valiantly on the battlefield that the common man believed that angels had descended from the heavens to help our army. How else could we have held our ground, how else could we have saved Lahore from falling to the enemy except with divine intervention? We were determined to win.

However, the world had other plans for us. The United States was mired in its own war in Vietnam. Amidst mounting international pressure, mainly from the United States and The Soviet Union, we were forced to accept a ceasefire that in the autumn of 1965. Our government told us that we were winning, and had the war continued, we would have won. On the other side of the border, the Indians believed the same. As expected, truth had been one of the first casualties of war, so each side continued believing what it wanted. Reluctantly we agreed to the cease-fire on September 22nd, 1965, a day after India did. On Zainab's orders, Jameela and Lal Khan removed the newspaper coverings from the windows and scrubbed the glass panes with kerosene to dissolve the black paint. However even a few months later, some of the windows in the neighbors' houses were still blacked out and the underground shelters where civilians had hidden during bomb raids had still not been bolted.

The sun had passed its zenith on the morning of the 25th of December, and Haji Rahmat had settled into his armchair in the library with his tea and newspaper. Nadia sat across from him at his desk, coloring in the cartoons on the comics page. September's *Time* magazine lay atop a pile of books, its cover yet another reminder of a war that had ended less than three months ago. "New War in Asia, Pakistan's Ayub Vs. India's Shastri" the cover page screamed. Silver scimitars separated the headshots of the nations' heads of states, stern and austere, even though the battle had been fought with tanks.

"Will India attack us again?" Nadia asked her father. She had finished coloring her comics and was glancing at the magazine on the desk. Haji Rahmat folded his newspaper and set it on the table beside him, holding his arms out for his daughter. She ran to him, curled into his lap, and buried her face in his chest.

"Don't you worry about a thing," he said stroking her hair. "It may. But we are brave. Do you know what the world is saying?"

Nadia shook her head no and smiled up at her father. He continued.

"Newspapers and journalists all over are saying that they have never seen a group of soldiers as confident and victorious as the Pakistanis. That for our soldiers, playing with fire is like playing with marbles." Nadia sat thoughtfully for a moment. "Don't you worry, beta. We will be alright." Haji Rahmat drew his arms tighter around his daughter.

Nadia seemed to consider her father's words before she jumped off the chair. "I'm hungry," she said. "Abbu, do you want a biscuit?"

Haji Rahmat smiled and shook his head no, and Nadia scampered off into the kitchen.

***

In the kitchen, two enamel jars sat on the counter in their usual spot next to the orange juicer. Nadia reached for the smaller jar, unscrewed the lid, and retrieved three chocolate biscuits, flower-shaped with a chocolate button.

A little boy of about ten sat glumly in the corner by the kitchen door.

"Hello," Nadia said brightly to the boy. "What is your name?"

Jameela reached into the china cabinet and retrieved a stack of plates. "His name is Nisar. He is my nephew."

"Hello, Nisar. Why are you sitting there in the corner?" Nadia prompted. The boy stared at the biscuit she was eating, and then glanced down at his dirty shirt.

"Are you hungry?" Nadia asked.

Nisar said nothing.

"Well, here I can share with you." She handed a biscuit to him. His face brightened. He took the chocolate flower biscuit and smiled shyly.

"Can't he talk?" Nadia asked Jameela.

"Yes, he can. But I've told him to be on his best behavior and keep his mouth shut. Otherwise, he talks too much and doesn't let me work." She turned to her nephew and prompted him. "Nisar, answer Baji."

Nisar immediately recited a rehearsed response, in English. "My name is Nisar. I am glad to meet you. Thanks very much."

"You're welcome," Nadia said. "But why are you sitting in the corner?" she pressed.

Again, Jameela responded, "So he can stay out of trouble."

"Do you want to play with us?" Nadia asked him. "We are going to pick jamuns."

Nisar looked up at his aunt, who nodded. "Go play with Baji. But come back in half an hour so you can help me sweep the kitchen. We have guests coming tonight for dinner."

Nadia skipped to the back garden, followed by Nisar who looked delighted at the prospect of having some respite from Jameela's watchful eye. Junaid was already up in the jamun tree, his lips purple from the juice of the berries.

"Nadia," he shouted when he saw his sister. "Pick up that basket, I'll throw down some jamuns for you."

Nadia immediately transferred her responsibility to Nisar and handed him the wicker basket. "Wait down here and hold the basket," she said. "I will climb up the tree and toss the jamuns to you. Make sure you catch them all."

With those words, Nadia disappeared into the leafy canopy. The leaves rustled as the children reached out for the glittering gems and tossed them below. Nisar leapt around the base of the tree catching the jamuns that rained from the sky and the children shrieked in delight, impressed with his speed. When they had two baskets full, Nadia and Junaid climbed back down, and the three of them sat under the shade of the tree, eating the fruit, staining their fingers and lips crimson.

"Let's take the rest inside for Ammi and Abbu," Junaid said, and they gathered their booty and made their way toward the kitchen.

***

60

A ruckus was in progress outside the front gate. Boisterous singing and clapping floated onto the driveway and there was no mistaking who had paid us a visit.

They always came in bands, the hijras. Dressed in festive, brightly colored women's clothing, they usually came to places where there had been a recent birth or marriage, to bless the home and request charity in return. I wondered how they had chanced upon us, and who had misinformed them.

"Go away, no one is home, and there is no celebration here to benefit from," Lal Khan hollered from behind the gate and continued sweeping the driveway.

From my vantage point, I could see them on the other side of the iron gate, a group of about five, laughing and singing, flattening their palms and pressing them together in loud claps. A heavily made-up face, with red lipstick and a glittering nose ring, peered through the wrought iron bars.

"What other celebration is needed when life itself is a celebration!" they quipped cheerfully upon spotting Lal Khan. "We aren't asking for your kingdom, just a little charity."

Lal Khan ignored them.

"May you be blessed with beautiful children, even in old age," the one with red lipstick offered.

"Oh, he isn't that old. He is young still!" their companion called out. "Come on now, handsome, don't turn us away empty-handed."

The children, their lips and fingertips still stained purple, came running towards the gate and watched with curiosity and a little trepidation. Zainab emerged from the kitchen door with money and called to her children. Nadia ran up to her mother and hugged her tight.

"Ammi, why are they here?" she asked.

"They just want money."

"Why do they look like that? Are they boys or girls?" she probed.

"Neither beta" Zainab smoothed her daughter's hair. They're hijras."

"How come?" Nadia asked.

"That's how Allah made them," Zainab replied.

"Do they kidnap little children?" Nadia questioned nervously.

"My friend told me they take away babies," Nisar blurted.

"No, no. Don't be silly." Zainab answered. "They don't kidnap anyone."

Nisar volunteered his own information, "They just come to see if the baby is like them. If it is, then they take it."

Nadia looked horrified at Nisar's words; and opened her mouth to question him further, when her brother spoke up.

"Why do they wear lipstick if they're boys?" Junaid asked.

Nadia's desire to correct her brother distracted her, and she turned to him with sass.

"They're not boys Junaid, they're hijras." she explained. "Did you not hear Ammi?"

Zainab glanced at her daughter in amusement. "All right. Enough. You are both such a mess. Go on, take a bath and get ready. I've laid your new clothes on the bed. Uncle Jee, Abbu's business partner, is coming to dinner. You need to be decent."

Zainab called out to Lal Khan and handed him several rupee notes. "Here, give them this money and send them off, Lal Khan."

Lal Khan walked over towards her shaking his head, "Baji, the more you give them the more often they will come."

"Oh Lal Khan. We shouldn't upset them. Allah listens to their prayers. And we don't want them to get upset and curse us! Please make them leave. Oh, and do put away that broom, our dinner guests will be arriving soon."

***

In the kitchen, Zainab tasted the biryani for salt and added the finishing touches on the dishes Khansama had prepared: a sprig of cilantro and some fried garlic on the daal, a sprinkle of cumin on the yogurt. She popped into the dining room and passed a cursory glance over the table, the sideboard, and the tea trolley. She adjusted the table settings and the embroidered table linens, and rearranged the roses in the crystal vase that sat in the center of the dining table.

Outside, the hijras had stopped singing, but they had not left. They had found a shady spot to the right of the front gate and stretched out comfortably on the footpath under the shade of the neem trees for a siesta. When, an hour later, Uncle Jee's car rolled up to our front gate, the leader of the group got up, and refreshed by their nap, sashayed up to the car with great enthusiasm. The rest of the group clapped and cheered in encouragement.

Lal Khan was embarrassed that the guests had arrived, and he had not managed to get the hijras to leave. He stepped outside, careful to close the gate behind him.

"I told you to leave, you shameless fool," he said. "I already gave you money."

"*Hai*, who are you calling *fool*? My name is Mehek, thank you." They responded curtly and turned with flair toward Uncle Jee's red Mercedes.

"Wah. Zabardast. What a car! Is the King of England arriving?" Mehek's head titled coquettishly and the hijras laughed at the joke.

The cheering companions bolstered Mehek's confidence, and they in turn knocked persistently at the window, offering strings of prayers and leaving greasy thumbprints on the glass.

From the back seat, Uncle Jee rolled down his window and issued a threat.

"Get your people away from here, or I'll have to call the police."

Used to such threats, Mehek answered without missing a beat. "Don't turn us away like this. Give us something, and we'll give you prayers. May you be successful, and may God give you beautiful cars like this one in every color."

"I said no, didn't I? I don't need your prayers," Uncle Jee

responded, irritated.

Mehek feigned mock horror, bright red lips parted in an exaggerated O. "Hai, such a beautiful car, and such an ugly heart."

Uncle Jee rolled up the window, almost crushing the hijra's hands in the process.

"Well, goodbye King of England," Mehek joked. "No need to call the police. We were just leaving." And with an exaggerated flick of the wrist and hand on the hip, the leader went back to the group, where they were greeted by song and dance. Then the group got up and wandered to the next street over.

Lal Khan opened the front gates and the red Mercedes swung into the driveway. He apologized profusely as he escorted the guests to the front door where Haji Rahmat and Zainab were waiting to receive them.

***

Uncle Jee was a middle-aged man of average height with thinning hair. His oval face was dissected by a bulbous nose and nostrils that flared when he smiled. He wore a well-pressed olive-green suit, a cream shirt, and brown loafers. A teal-colored pocket square peered out of the coat pocket. In each hand, he carried a substantial gift bag. His wife, Rabab, was, dressed like a younger woman would be, in a short blue shirt and fashionable bell-bottoms. She carried herself gracefully and smelled expensive, of lavender and jasmine buds collected at dawn.

"It's such a pleasure to have you over." Zainab welcomed them with a smile.

"The pleasure is ours," Uncle Jee replied.

"What a beautiful home, with such character. I love the yellow stone." Rabab's compliment pleased me tremendously, and I thought to myself, here is a woman of good taste.

"Indeed," added Uncle Jee. "A lovely home. But where are the youngsters?" His narrowing eyes searched the drawing room, as though expecting the children to be hiding behind the scooped wooden chairs in the corner of the room.

"Oh, they made a mess eating jamuns," Zainab laughed. "I've sent them to bathe. They will be here soon."

"Wonderful," Uncle Jee said, setting the two bags onto the kidney-shaped coffee table. "I have gifts for them."

Zainab glanced at the festively wrapped boxes that peeked out of the brown bags. "You really shouldn't have," she protested. "You'll spoil them."

"Oh, it's nothing," Uncle Jee responded. "We have no children, so I have nothing to do but to spoil yours!" He handed Haji Rahmat a bag. "Here, this is for you."

Haji Rahmat peered inside. "Aray, you know we don't drink here," he said.

"Come on, I thought you'd make an exception for special occasions. We're celebrating a big project launch," Uncle Jee said.

"Not a chance. It was my wedding promise to the wife. She wouldn't marry me until I promised." And he grinned at Zainab.

Zainab smiled. "Rabab, can I offer you some fresh juice?" she asked. "Best oranges of the season."

"Thank you, but I'm alright," Rabab answered. "I must save room for dinner. I hear you're an excellent cook."

"I'll take a glass of orange juice," Uncle Jee said. "Since Haji Rahmat won't share a drink of vodka with me." He sat down comfortably on the sofa; one leg crossed over the other and took a sip of the cold drink.

Presently, Jameela brought in the children, clean in their pressed outfits with hair neatly brushed.

"Nadia has grown since I saw her last! And Junaid! Soon your handsome son will be ready to take over the business!" Rabab said.

Haji Rahmat laughed, a hearty laugh that rose deep from the belly. The children smiled.

"Come sit with me, Nadia," Uncle Jee said. "I have something for you." Nadia skipped over to Uncle Jee, who sat her on his lap and presented her with a lavish box wrapped in shiny red paper.

The four-year-old's eyes widened in anticipation and excitement. She clutched the box and looked up at her mother. "May I unwrap it?" she asked.

"Of course you may," Uncle Jee boomed. Zainab smiled and nodded. Within twenty seconds, the box was unwrapped, and Nadia shrieked in delight to see a fancy doll with blonde coiffed hair, a pink dress, and a red fur-trimmed satin coat.

"What do we say, beta?" Zainab prodded.

"A Barbie!" Nadia screamed, beside herself with joy. "Everybody in school wants this! I can't believe I have it. Thank you, thank you!" She leapt off Uncle Jee's lap and ran to show her mother the doll.

"This is all the rage," Aunty quipped. "Every girl wants a Magnificence Barbie!"

Nadia gasped in happiness as she ran her fingers along the pink chiffon skirt and the satin jacket. Then it was Junaid's turn. He received a large remote-controlled car, which made his eyes widen in joyful surprise. "Oh, first-rate!" he said. "Thank you, Uncle Jee and Aunty."

I was surprised at the extravagance of these foreign toy gifts during a time while we were still recoiling from war and most people's businesses were not doing as well.

Haji Rahmat helped him put in the batteries. He zoomed the car around the floor, under the table, and around the chairs.

After a while, Zainab noticed the time.

"It's almost eight-thirty," she said. "Children, it's time for bed now."

Junaid scowled. "May I stay and eat kulfi with the guests, please?" he asked.

Haji Rahmat shook his head. "No. It's too late for dessert. Besides your Quran teacher will be here early in the morning tomorrow. Off to bed now, both of you."

Zainab led the children out as the guests settled to dinner. She practically had to carry Nadia out of the room, doll, wrapping paper scraps, excitement and all.

Over dinner that evening, new business partnerships were formed and promises made; and only time would tell how devastating or fruitful this would be. Uncle Jee became an investor in Haji Rahmat's new business.

As 1965 drew to a close, New Year's Eve was celebrated with cautionary hope and muted enthusiasm. I considered the events of the past year and hoped the worst was over. I suppose we did have something to celebrate, we may not have won the war, but *not losing* a war warrants some celebration after all.

11

January 1967

After the festivities of New Year's Eve subsided, January marked the end of the winter holidays—and much to the children's dismay the start of the school year brought routines. The afternoons previously spent blissfully reading, or playing cricket or hopscotch, would now be spent in the library completing lessons. It was one such Monday afternoon in 1967 when Nadia and Junaid were sprawled on the oversized Turkish rug in the library, surrounded by backpacks, and books that Nisar peeked in. He had become a permanent addition to the household staff. When Zainab found out that Jameela was going to send him to apprentice in a mechanic's workshop to earn money to support his family, she felt sorry for the little boy, and offered him employment. Mostly, he forgot the few chores that were assigned to him, as is expected of a ten-year-old boy, and Jameela was often seen twisting his ear and calling him names. But he became part of the family: a part-time assistant for Jameela and a part-time companion for the children.

"Come, let's play cricket," Nisar said sticking his head in through the library door that had been left ajar.

Nadia glanced up from an illustrated copy of *Poems for Children*. She had just begun Class 1 and felt extremely proud that she too, like her older brother, had homework. "We can't play with you," she said. "We are really busy. Now that I'm getting older, I also have homework to do."

Nisar's lips drooped in disappointment.

"Why don't you have any homework?" Nadia called out, the surprise apparent in her voice.

Nisar stood in the door frame and shrugged.

"Well, don't just stand there. Come here, do some of my homework for me," she ordered.

Nisar shifted his feet, uncomfortable. "I'll do it wrong, then your teacher will scold you," he mumbled.

Nadia gestured to him to come in. "Oh, come here! It's really easy. Look. You just read this and copy it three times. Come on. Help me."

Nisar walked over to the children and sat down, cross-legged on the edge of the rug. Nadia handed him a small, yellow, bound notebook.

"Here, do this," she said and pointed to the neatly written sentences she was supposed to copy.

Nisar stared at the page, running his finger back and forth over the words.

Nadia handed him a freshly sharpened pencil and urged him to begin.

"I don't know how to write ... or read," he said softly, a few minutes later.

"Don't lie. It's a big sin." Nadia sharpened her own pencil into a point.

"I'm not lying," Nisar stammered.

"Nadia, please can you just stop talking," Junaid said. "Thirteen times nine is ... argh! I keep forgetting my mental math."

Nadia ignored her brother. "Why can't you read?" she asked Nisar.

"No one taught me."

Nadia didn't look like she believed him. "What were you doing at school, then?"

"I ran away from school," Nisar said. "The teachers would beat me."

"You ran away?" she said, sounding a little horrified but mostly impressed by his courage.

"Wish I could run away from school," Junaid said. "Mr. Goveas canes us. He is awful." He finished his last math problem and snapped his book shut. "Nadia, you're lucky. They don't cane the girls; they just give them extra homework."

"I don't get caned because I always do the right thing," Nadia answered and tossed her hair behind her neck.

Junaid raised an eyebrow at his sister and shook his head.

"Anyway," Nadia turned her attention back to Nisar. "Look here," she said. "I will teach you. It isn't hard. Repeat after me." She pointed to the open book in front of her and began reciting. *"I wandered lonely as a cloud."*

"I vonderd lon ly ... " Nisar blushed as he struggled to repeat the words.

"No, no!" Nadia said. "Say the words correctly. Watch how I say it, *I wandered lonely."*

Nisar repeated, his teeth pressed on his lower lip, making the w harsh and awkward: "I vonderd lonely."

Nadia shook her head. "Okay. Watch my mouth. Look at how my mouth goes. W. W. Wandered." She put her lips together as though whistling.

Nisar grimaced, embarrassed. "That's what I am saying. *Vonderd."*

Nadia shook her head. "Oh ho! You have to practice *a lot.* But you will get it. Rami, my friend in class, he is a terrible reader. Kind of like you. But Mrs. Joseph helps him, and I will help you."

For the next few minutes, the children laughed and made fun of each other, as their books lay forgotten. Then Jameela called out to Nisar, and he rushed to the kitchen, leaving the children to finish their homework.

Later that evening, as Zainab tucked her children into bed, Nadia shared Nisar's issue with her mother.

"Ammi, I have to tell you a secret," she began.

"What is the matter?"

Nadia whispered, "Nisar doesn't know how to read."

Junaid popped his head in through the bathroom the children shared and responded. "That's not even a secret."

Zainab gave Nadia a kiss on the forehead and covered her feet with a blanket. "Is that right? Well, many people don't know how to read. You're very lucky."

Nadia kicked her blanket off. "It's too hot for a blanket," she said. "Nisar told me he used to run away from school."

"Yes, that is what Jameela told me, too."

"Well, send him back to school then," the precocious five-year-old answered. "Abbu always says, running away is not the answer."

"He is ten and can't read. No school will take him now."

It was quiet for a few minutes. Zainab turned the bedside lamp off and got up from Nadia's bed. "Goodnight my loves. Junaid, off to bed with you."

"Wait, wait. I have an idea," Nadia said. "I'm going to be his reading teacher. But it might be a bit hard. He is very poor at reading. C minus."

Junaid laughed from the doorway. "Nisar will run away again. You're so bossy."

Nadia rolled her eyes at her brother. "No one asked you, dumbo."

"Nadia. Please don't speak to your brother that way," Zainab said. She continued with a smile. "That's a good idea. I'm sure you will make a wonderful teacher. In fact, what I will do is hire a teacher who can come and teach him in the morning while you both are at school. This way he can catch up. You can help him in the afternoon, but only after you are done with your lessons. But now, bedtime. No more talking."

Nadia hugged her mother in excitement, incredibly pleased with her new responsibility. When her mother left the room, she jumped out of bed and sat on her desk, scribbling notes about what she would teach Nisar.

The very next day after school, Nadia who had herself recently learned to read, held her first reading lesson with Nisar. She was exuberant with pride at her new responsibility, taking care to set up her standing blackboard in the library, beginning with a simple lesson *Peter and Jane*, book number 1A and giving Nisar encouraging affirmations like a kind old teacher would. Lessons with the tutor that Zainab hired began a few weeks later. Nisar, though deflated about the prospect of a tutor every morning, resigned himself to learning to read—not because he was delighted to learn, but because he did not want to embarrass himself and disappoint Nadia.

12

July 1967

Nisar was a fast learner, and Nadia took her self-imposed job very seriously. Once a week she tested him on his reading, giving him golden star stickers if he did well. One gusty afternoon, in the summer of 1967, as Nadia tested her student on his reading in the library, the warm wind picked up, and along with the bits of debris and dust dispersed the rumor that Fatima Jinnah, the sister of our country's founder, had been found dead in her home that morning.

Lal Khan's radio was on, and inside Haji Rahmat waited for the news on the television. A special broadcast confirmed the rumors; the Mother of the Nation, as she was fondly known, had died of a heart attack peacefully in her residence. More details would follow in the evening news.

At five p.m., the evening newspaper, tightly rolled and secured with a rubber band flew in over the gate and landed with a thud on the driveway like a dead bird.

"Scoundrel!" Lal Khan shouted to the newspaper boy on the other side of the gate, who had already cycled away. "How many times do I need to tell you, ring the bell and leave the paper at the gate. You'll kill me one of these days." He bent down and picked the paper up and walked over to the back garden.

Khansama was setting tea out on the wrought iron table in the garden. Haji Rahmat and Zainab conversed with Uncle Jee and

Aunty Rabab, while the children played hopscotch.

"Ah. Thank you, Lal Khan," Haji Rahmat slid the rubber band off the paper and smoothed it out. Lal Khan took a step back and lingered to hear some updates on Fatima Jinnah's death.

"It says here that she died of a heart attack," he said scanning the headlines. "Nothing more than what we heard on the radio."

"What is the point of the paper then?" mused Lal Khan. "I don't believe it was a heart attack. I heard she was seen at a wedding the night before looking in tip-top shape."

"Who told you?" Haji Rahmat questioned.

"My cousin's nephew. He works next door to Mohatta Palace. He suspects foul play."

"I wouldn't be surprised," Haji Rahmat mused.

"What a loss," Zainab said sadly and recited the prayer for the deceased. The rest joined in.

"She was one of the good ones, wasn't she," Aunty Rabab sighed. "It's hard when we lose the good ones."

"The government didn't trust her," Uncle Jee said after a long slurp of tea. "They accused her of being a traitor."

"That's to be expected," Haji Rahmat said. "She ran against Ayub for president. It was his way to defame her. Anyhow since when do we believe our government?" It was part of Haji Rahmat's breed of patriotism, to be ever suspicious of the government.

"I was hoping she would somehow run for president again. I'm still sad she lost the election. When is the funeral?" Zainab asked.

Haji Rahmat looked up from the paper. "Tomorrow," he answered.

"Did they agree to let her be buried in the Mazaar, as she had requested?"

"They had to. A protest broke out when the officials decided to do otherwise," Lal Khan interjected.

Haji Rahmat nodded. "It says so here." He read out the newspaper. "*Mohtarma Fatima Jinnah will be laid to rest next to her brother The Quaid-e-Azam."*

Death; always an unwelcome reminder of the temporary nature of our lives. The news of Fatima Jinnah's death reminded me how the city had been weighted by disappointment when she had lost the presidential election to Ayub Khan just two years ago, in 1965. Everyone had rallied behind her, believing in her, so sure that she would win and bring back Mohammad Ali Jinnah's vision to our country. Although she won the popular vote, she lost the electoral, and though many blamed vote-rigging; she conceded to Ayub Khan with dignity.

The melodious voice of the street ice lolly seller advertising the new chocobar disrupted my thoughts. His voice floated over the front gate, down the driveway, and towards the back.

Junaid's ears perked up. "The ice lolly man is here! Abbu, please, can we get some?" His eyes pleaded at his father and added. "It's so very hot."

"Yes, please please please, Abbu?" Nadia leaped up in excitement.

Uncle Jee answered before Haji Rahmat or Zainab could. "Yes, you certainly may. I'll come with you, let's get some ice lollies."

Nadia and Junaid cheered. "Thank you, Uncle Jee, you're the best!" They raced ahead in excitement, calling out to Lal Khan.

"Stop him, Lal Khan, stop the ice lolly man."

Uncle Jee laughed his big-bellied laugh and got up to follow the children. Lal Khan opened the gate and hollered, and the ice lolly man rambled to our gate with his makeshift cart; a hefty metal icebox strapped onto a dolly with wheels. He parked his cart at the gate, and the children stepped out with Uncle Jee.

"What will you have?" the ice lolly man asked. "Orange ice lolly, kulfi, or chocobar?"

"One orange lolly for me," Junaid said.

The ice lolly man unwrapped the fluorescent orange frozen treat and handed it to Junaid.

"And for the little miss?"

"You have the new chocobar?" Nadia shouted with excitement. "I can't believe you have the chocobar!"

"I do! Brand new. Mazaydaar!" He pulled a chocolate-covered ice cream bar out of the icebox and showed it to her.

Nadia's eyes glittered with joy, but then she covered her face with her hands, disconcerted at having to make a decision. "Whatever shall I do? I want both so badly. Orange and chocobar. How can I decide between my two favorites?"

"Go ahead, get both," Uncle Jee said, laughing. "No need to pick one."

"No, she cannot! Uncle Jee, Ammi says we can only have one." Junaid said while he slurped on his lolly with satisfaction. Nadia pouted.

"Let me try yours," she said to her brother. "So I can decide."

"Get your own, Nadia. I'm not sharing."

The six-year-old peered inside the icebox, staring longingly at the stripes of orange, chocolate, and cream. Beads of condensation were forming on the outside of the metal icebox and trickling down the side.

"Has the miss decided?" the ice lolly man asked Nadia. "I can't keep the box open for so long, beta. Everything will melt."

"She will have one of each," Uncle Jee said to the ice lolly man. "I made the decision for her."

Nadia looked up, incredulous. "Really?"

"Ammi said only *one*." Junaid reminded Uncle Jee and turned to his sister. "Nadia, don't be so greedy."

"Well, your Ammi isn't here. This is your Uncle Jee's treat! Don't worry, I won't tell your Ammi. This is our secret!" He winked and laughed.

Nadia did not need any more convincing. She gave Uncle Jee an exuberant hug and immediately acquired an orange lolly in her right hand and a chocobar in her left. She skipped along to the front veranda, settled herself comfortably on steps, and began to unwrap the treats.

"Junaid, you too, go ahead, take another one," Uncle Jee said and handed the ice lolly man some crisp rupee notes.

"What a nice uncle you got there," the ice lolly seller said and handed Junaid a chocobar. He retrieved a jute pouch from the inside of his kurta pocket, counted the change, and handed some coins back to Uncle Jee.

Junaid joined his sister on the steps, Lal Khan locked the front gate, and the ice lolly man retreated down the street. Uncle Jee walked to the back garden to join the adults and I noticed for the first time that he walked with a little limp in his right foot. I wondered if it was too prudish of me to think that Uncle Jee was slightly out of line in sidestepping Zainab's rules. He had a tendency to do that; to spoil the children with extravagant gifts, encourage them to do things that Zainab normally wouldn't allow, slip them treats here and there, and through these actions, he cemented his position as the children's favorite uncle.

Fatima Jinnah was laid to rest the next day. The men of the household attended; Junaid and Nisar went too, and Zainab, Nadia, and Jameela followed the coverage on television. The procession gained strength as it marched from her home in Clifton to the Quaid's burial mazaar in the center of the city. At every street, the hordes thickened, and the steady hum of *"Pakistan Zindabad,"* and *"Long Live Madr-e-Millat"* resounded from the earth and lingered in the sky, echoing in every corner. The women climbed to the tops of buildings in the path of the funeral procession and tossed rose petals on the crowds below. At the burial site, when the mourners tried to come close to her body for viewing and to pay respects, they were stopped. A riot ensued; for how could the police stop the people from paying their respects to the Mother of our Nation? The crowds were held back with batons and tear gas, and no one was allowed to come close to the body.

When Fatima Jinnah was finally buried, we felt an irreparable loss, of things that once were but would never be again.

13

July 1968

On a Sunday evening, after the family came home from a dinner at Uncle Jee's house, Nadia walked towards her bedroom, with a troubled, distracted look on her face. Nisar called out to her as she walked past the kitchen, informing her proudly that he had finished the book she had assigned to him for reading, and asked if she would like to test him. She walked past him without as much as turning in his direction, as though she hadn't even heard him. He looked puzzled, and with a shrug of disappointment continued wiping down the kitchen counters.

Once in her bedroom, Nadia shut the door and locked it. She sat on her bed for a few minutes and then opened the bottom drawer of her wardrobe and pulled out her Magnificent Barbie. She turned and glanced around surreptitiously, as though to make sure no one was watching her, and then ripped off the doll's lovely chiffon skirt. Suddenly upset at what she had done, she shoved the doll back in the drawer and slammed the drawer shut. For a moment, she looked guilty and a tinge of sadness dulled her eyes. Then she took a pen from her desk, opened the drawer again, and scribbled over the doll's face and the drawer too, with so much intensity that the point of the pen made grooves in the wood. With a pair of scissors, she hacked off the doll's soft blonde hair.

She sat there for a few minutes, her expression blank. I saw her little shoulders tense up as fear made its way through her frame.

Perhaps realization dawned on her, that she would be in trouble for ruining her expensive doll. She wrapped it up in a brown paper bag and hid it under her bed behind the extra blanket. Later that night, when everyone was asleep, she got out of bed and threw her doll in the kitchen trash, making sure to conceal it under the onion peels, orange rinds, and crusty bread ends. The next morning, the garbage truck took Nadia's secret out with the day's trash to be burned at the collection point.

14

It has been six weeks since Haji Rahmat's funeral and much longer since I have undergone any structural improvements of consequence. The marble name plaque, *Manzil-e-Azadi*, which Haji Rahmat had proudly displayed at the front gate, is dulled by smog, and a discernible crack splits it down the middle. The wood on the windows is sun-bleached, and in desperate need of refinishing. Not that I am assigning any blame for this negligence—I know it is inappropriate to think about maintenance and renovations when we have just had a death in the household.

Zainab is in her bedroom. The curtains are pulled to the side and the glass panes are open; the wire-mesh netting keeps mosquitoes out. The jasmine hedges outside are blooming today and tiny white flowers peer in.

"I'm going to go through Abbu's clothes," Zainab says to Junaid, who has just walked into her room. "Maybe I should give some things away."

Junaid follows his mother into her dressing room. Haji Rahmat's cupboards, situated at the back end of the room, are open. Stacks of clothes lay on the floor. The sight of all his things laid out this way is unsettling.

"I'll help you," he says. "I'll get the boxes down."

Junaid drags a small wooden step stool to the closet, careful not to knock over the neat piles Zainab has made. On the top shelves, there are boxes of varying dimensions, stacked by size in an orderly fashion. One by one, he retrieves the boxes and places them on the ground.

The first is a hatbox made of stiff, yellowed cardboard. Inside sits a karakul cap. It is black and woolen, slightly worn around the edges, and scented with memory: agarwood, salt in the air, and early morning dew. I remember it well, Haji Rahmat was wearing it the day he and Zainab first arrived at the property that November day in 1957. Junaid lifts it out and tries it on, like he used to when he was eight, and would pretend to be his father and order the house staff around. Zainab can't help but smile. "That was his favorite, a gift from your grandfather," she says. "I want to keep it."

Junaid smiles and puts the cap back into the box. He opens the next box, a rectangular cardboard one wrapped in velvet. Inside is a young woman's wedding outfit, cream-colored silk with tiny pearls and intricate gold embroidery.

Zainab's face wilts. "Oh. So that's where he hid Nadia's wedding dress," she whispers running her fingers over the pearls. "After the wedding was called off, I couldn't bear to see it, but couldn't bear to get rid of it either," her voice cracks. "So your father kept it away from me."

I know Junaid does not want to start a discussion on Nadia's wedding. He replaces the lid on the box quickly and returns it to the closet.

"Do you want tea? Or some fruit?" he asks. "I can ask Nisar to bring some up for you." He is trying to distract his mother. Zainab shakes her head no, and so they begin to go through the closet and create more piles in the corner: shirts, pants, kurtas, and sherwanis. I wish they didn't have to do this, not yet at least.

"Maybe one day she will wear it still," Zainab says.

Junaid smiles, and nods. Zainab sits on the step stool, folding clothes as though folding spiderwebs, as though afraid of dislodging or losing memories. Junaid stands next to her and stares out the window. There is a tear in the mesh netting, and I wonder if he notices.

"He wasn't supposed to die yet," she says and smooths the creases in the pants she is folding. "Not before he saw you both married, not before seeing his grandchildren."

Junaid turns and bends down to face his mother and holds her hand in his. "I know, Ammi," he whispers. The dressing room feels smaller than usual, suffocating.

"It's what people say, you know, that makes it worse," Zainab says, suddenly. "The pity they feel for me. I can't take it. Poor Zainab, they say. God has given her so much, but all her money cannot cure her daughter. I can't listen to that anymore."

"Ammi. Nobody says that. And even if they do, it doesn't matter." He pauses, as though wondering what to say next. "Soon someone else will pass away, or someone's daughter will elope, or someone's house will be broken into. And people will move on to the next story."

Zainab opens a drawer. She runs her fingers over the neat rows of ties and cufflinks. "They may move on," she says. "But will Nadia get better?"

Junaid doesn't know. I don't know either.

"Have you seen her this morning?" Zainab asks. "She didn't come out for breakfast."

Junaid shakes his head; there is sorrow in his eyes and the burden of unspoken words.

***

Nadia is in her room as usual. Her shoulder-length hair is not brushed. She is sitting on her bed, scribbling in her notebook. Her nails have been bitten back. She has been up all night, copying pages from A *History of Botany*. She has even traced the illustrations. The curtains are drawn but her bedside lamp shines. Shards of daylight that creep in from under her bedroom door cast shadows over her face, her torso, and the bed covers. Nadia stops writing and scans around the room. She searches in her bedside drawer, under her pillow, and on the floor, frantic as though missing something of vital importance. Unable to find what she wants; she runs to her desk. The eraser is there. With great conviction, she erases the entire last page she has copied: the description of the *Mentha asiatica* and the sketches of the mint plant. She sits at her table and rewrites the words, careful to get the curves of the letters correct, and the spacing consistent. Then she begins the drawing, careful to get the tiny, jagged leaves just right. Finally satisfied, she closes her notebook and places it on top of the pile of books on her desk. She walks back to her bed. A yellow blister pack sits on her bedside table. She presses one pill out and swallows it with a gulp of water. Then she curls under her blanket, like a worm, and goes to sleep.

At three p.m., Nurse D' Souza will come. Then Apa will come to perform a prayer. It won't matter. She doesn't get better.

15

September 1968

It happened on a Monday afternoon in 1968.
It had been an hour since the children had come back from school. Khansama was clearing up the remnants of a delicious lunch from the table when Uncle Jee and Aunty Rabab dropped in.

"What a nice surprise," Zainab said and welcomed them into the sitting room. "Uncle Jee, you're not at work today?"

"I had some business at the bank, so I left work early. I have some papers for Haji Rahmat to sign," Uncle Jee answered.

"Oh, Haji is not home. But I was just going to have some tea. Please join me."

Zainab asked Khansama to bring in tea and led the guests into the sitting room, where she cracked open the French doors to the patio and turned on the standing fan.

"It's so very hot today," she said, fanning her face with her hand. "We need some rain. How is your family, Rabab?" she asked.

Aunty Rabab patted her face delicately with a napkin. "They are well, thank you."

Uncle Jee sat down on the sofa and set an envelope of papers on the table. These are for Haji Rahmat," he said. "I think congratulations are in order on the new business venture. We are very fortunate to have received the funding."

Zainab smiled. "Thank you. To you as well. I am so glad the

project is off to such a good start."

Khansama brought in a tray of potato samosas and tea from the kitchen and set it on the coffee table. Uncle Jee reached over for a plate.

"Tell me, Zainab," Aunty Rabab began. "Is it true what I heard about Bisma's daughter?"

Zainab colored a little at the mention of her niece back in India. "What have you heard?" she asked.

"Well, that she fell in love with a Hindu boy and eloped?"

Zainab gave Aunty Rabab a tight-lipped smile. "Well, I hope he is a good boy and keeps her happy. What more can I say, really?"

Aunty Rabab raised her eyebrows, unsympathetic, and shook her head. "May God protect our kids."

Uncle Jee placed his plate back on the tea trolley and brushed a few crumbs off his shirt. "I'll leave you ladies to your chatter," he said and got up. "Take a stroll, if I may."

Uncle Jee walked through the French doors to the patio and circled around the front of the property to the side, toward the cricket pitch. He walked past the quarters where Lal Khan was saying his prayers. He peeked into the kitchen where Khansama was washing saucepans. Through the open window, Jameela was visible in the laundry room, doing the ironing. Uncle Jee walked slowly with his little limp towards the back.

The children were on the cricket pitch. Nadia stood by the wicket with her bat in hand waiting for Junaid to bowl.

"Hi Uncle Jee!" Junaid yelled from afar.

"How are my favorites?" Uncle Jee boomed as he walked up towards the children.

"Come play with us, Uncle Jee! Let's play hide-and-seek," Junaid said.

"Alright, if that's what Junaid wants, that's what we'll do. Let's play hide-and-seek. Junaid, you're it."

Nadia stared down at the ground and kicked the dirt with her feet.

"I don't want to play," she said. "We just started playing cricket and it's my turn to bat."

"Come on, be a good girl. Listen to your brother."

"Nadia, please! Don't be a spoilsport."

Nadia's forehead wrinkled with apprehension, and she bit nervously at her fingernail.

"Okay, I'm it. Go hide." Junaid turned to face the neem tree. "One. Two. Three ..."

"Nadia," Uncle Jee said. "Come with me. I know a good hiding place." He took Nadia's hand and led her to the storage room alongside the cricket pitch.

"Right here, this is a good place," Uncle Jee said and pushed open the wooden door.

"But I don't like the dark, this room is dark," Nadia said, almost in tears.

"We won't shut the door all the way, it won't be dark. Don't worry."

Nadia strained her neck to see if she could catch sight perhaps of Junaid. No one was around.

Uncle Jee and Nadia hid inside the dusty little room, and as Uncle Jee shut the door all the way, Nadia pleaded again, "I don't like the dark."

"You're safe here, don't worry," he responded.

Time moved slowly in the darkness of the storeroom.

Junaid ran past the storage shed to the front of the grounds, to search for his sister in her usual hiding places. He peeked into Lal Khan's quarters, checked behind the cars in the driveway, and ran up the steps to the front porch to see if she was crouching behind the oversized terra cotta pots. Disappointed, he paused for a few minutes and spun around. Then he made his way toward the storage shed.

Uncle Jee opened the door a crack.

Junaid spotted the door shift and yelled in excitement. "I know you're in there, I saw the door move!" He ran to the shed and kicked the door open, shouting, "Found you! Found you! My turn to hide now."

Uncle Jee laughed, his shirt rumpled over his belly, but Nadia stumbled out, her face flush and tight. Head down, she pushed past Junaid and ran toward the kitchen.

"Nadia, where are you going?" Junaid asked. "It is my turn to hide!"

His sister did not turn back but kept running, her dark hair streaming behind her.

"Spoilsport!" he called out, but Nadia sprinted to the kitchen door. Her arms strained at the weight as she yanked it open. She stopped abruptly, the heavy door swinging shut behind her, and stood there in the middle of the kitchen, as though lost, unsure of where she was, and of where she had to go. Her eyes darted around like an injured gazelle, to the Formica cabinetry, the square yellow backsplash tiles, the kitchen sink filled with dishes, the wooden cutting board on the counter piled with bread ends.

Khansama came in with a tray of dirty teacups, whistling an old love song. "What's the matter?" he asked her, his eyes concerned at the sight of her distress.

"Where is Ammi?" she asked. But without waiting for an answer, she made her way to the living room, where her mother was chatting with Aunty Rabab. Seeing that her mother had company, she walked through the room quickly, with her head bent low, avoiding eye contact.

"Come here, Nadia," Zainab said. "Where are you going?"

Nadia raised her face to her mother. For a moment, she looked like she was going to say something, but then Uncle Jee came through the door. Junaid was with him, holding a big box of Cadbury Flake bars as if he carried a chest filled with gold. Nadia's body stiffened.

"What's the matter, Nadia?" Zainab asked. "Are you alright?"

"I think she's just upset because her hiding place was no good,"

Junaid volunteered. "And now she doesn't want to play with us anymore."

Nadia, mute, swept her eyes to her brother, and then quickly away again. Ignoring her, Junaid reached for a samosa, and in doing so knocked over the cup of tea that sat on the table. The hot liquid splashed on his bare leg and spilled on the rug. Junaid screamed in pain.

Aunty Rabab jumped up. "Bring ice, bring ice," she shouted and started dabbing towels on his leg.

Zainab called out to Jameela, to bring Burnol ointment and a cold towel. The tea had scalded the boy, leaving a red splotch just below his knee. And it had left a miserable brown stain on the rug and I knew it must have crossed Zainab's mind that tea stains are nearly impossible to dislodge from a cream-colored Persian rug.

Uncle Jee opened the box of Flake chocolate and handed Junaid three bars. He held a bright yellow Flake bar toward Nadia, saying, "Here you go, my dear."

Nadia blanched, her arms remaining at her side. After a beat, she turned around and ran from the room. My floors thrummed with the force of her footfalls as she raced to her bedroom, and across the room to her bed. She sat, in silence, stone-faced, not crying, barely breathing. Her only movement was the contortions making her eyes, her cheeks, her lips ripple: confusion, shame, and fear played across her face. It pained me to see her like this, impacted me forever. I had seen this discordant display of emotion before. That day the family had come back from Uncle Jee's residence just a few months ago, that day Nadia had cut off her Magnificent Barbie's hair.

Over the years, within my walls, I have heard terrible stories of the evil humans do to each other. The realization of what must have happened in that storage room today, and at Uncle Jee's a few months ago, seeped into my very foundation, with the revolting immediacy of the smell of sewage penetrating the air. I did not know what to do. Just as the rancid odor lingers, even after the sewage has been removed, thus it lingered now, the anger, the repulsion, and the horror. And most of all, the guilt of not being able to protect Nadia. Or tell anyone.

I thought of the day Uncle Jee had first come to visit us ... that day the hijras had stopped by. For that day when Uncle Jee's car had rolled up to my gates, their leader declared that Uncle Jee had an ugly heart. Could it be that they had been the only one to see Uncle Jee for who he really was?

***

That evening at dinnertime, Zainab found Nadia in her bed. The seven-year-old curled like a millipede beneath the blankets and refused to get out of bed, saying her stomach hurt. Jameela brought soup and tried to force Nadia to eat, but the child did not allow a morsel into her mouth and fell asleep without dinner.

That night, the wind was enraged. It whistled through the leaves, the whistling turning into roaring; it picked up gravel and rocks and hurled them over the grounds. It dislodged sheaths of the coconut palm and tossed them around the garden. Heavy branches of the neem and jamun whirled about in the air and hurtled across the patio leaving the wicker chairs and wrought iron table upturned. The noise woke up Zainab, who went to check on the children, and found Nadia with a high fever. She insisted that Nadia eat a biscuit and gave her Calpol. Then she carried her daughter to her bedroom and woke up Haji Rahmat.

"Keep an eye on her," she whispered. "Her fever is 102. I'll be right back."

Haji Rahmat wrapped his blanket around his daughter and held her shivering body close while Zainab went to the bathroom. She mixed ice-cold water and eau de cologne in a steel basin and soaked some muslin washcloths in it. She brought it to the bedside, and sat next to Nadia, squeezing the excess water out and layering the strips of muslin on her daughter's head to cool her body and bring the fever down. The soothing smell of Muelhenn's Cologne Number 4711 filled the room, and finally, at seven a.m.

when the fever broke, Nadia fell asleep.

While they slept, I felt the burden intensify. The u-pipe under the kitchen sink burst and water gushed out through the cabinets onto the marble floor. It seeped into the baseboards of the kitchen and, as the water level rose, it filled the lower wooden cabinets.

The next morning, members of the household awoke to gardens scattered with debris and branches, and a flooded kitchen. A plumber and a tree trimmer were sent for, to control the chaos that had erupted overnight.

Nadia's fever passed, but her flesh was a ghastly gray. It was not even ten a.m. and she had thrown up twice. Zainab wondered out loud what she had eaten the day before and Jameela listed everything from breakfast to dinner. They couldn't find a culprit, but Nadia couldn't even hold water down and refused to leave her bed, so Haji Rahmat returned home with a doctor that afternoon. Nadia burst into tears when she saw the doctor, and she recoiled in horror when he came near, insisting he would hurt her.

"No he won't, I promise, beta," Zainab said. "Look, he has no drips, no injections, he just wants to check your stomach." But the girl was nearly delirious, trying to get away from him, and Haji Rahmat and Zainab each held one hand to soothe her while the doctor checked her breathing, her stomach, and her throat. He misdiagnosed her condition as a stomach flu and prescribed a week-long course of Flagyl.

***

The tree cutter arrived early the following morning. All the fruit trees were situated along the far end of the property, and he began with the coconut trees that trimmed the back garden along the back wall. He relieved them of their heavy boughs and dry sheaths atop. Next, he moved on to the neem tree and snipped away to thin the foliage. The air smelled fragrant and fresh with the scent of bark and neem leaves. When the sun reached high in the sky, and it became too hot to work, he took his lunch and rested under the shade of the tree. Then, when the heat had lessened, he began working again, hoping to finish up his job before the sun set. He moved his ladder from the neem to the jamun tree situated at the back corner of the garden. He propped his ladder up against the trunk and disappeared into its leafy foliage. The jamuns glistened in the late afternoon light like little purple gems.

The tree cutter had been up there but a few minutes when we heard a scream, followed by the sound of snapping branches and twigs. Then a body, I imagine it was the tree cutter's because he was the only one there, dropped out of the leafy mass. There was a loud thud as he landed on the pile of leaves that had accumulated on the ground.

Lal Khan was on the chair outside his quarters enjoying late afternoon tea. The noise prompted him to set his cup down and, a little annoyed to be disturbed, he ventured to the back to see what had happened.

He was met halfway by the tree cutter, who was running toward the front gate, his face awash with confusion and fear.

"What's the matter?" Lal Khan asked. "Why are you running? What was that noise?"

"Something threw me off the tree!" he yelled. "Something threw me off the tree!'

Lal Khan stared. "Have you lost your mind?" he asked. "What are you talking about? Where are you going? You haven't finished the job! Do you not want to get paid?"

"I can't work here," the tree cutter said. "This place is possessed. Something threw me off that tree."

Nisar, who was washing the mops in the outdoor sinks, sensed some drama and looking for an opportunity for distraction, came over to see what the ruckus was.

The tree cutter turned around repeatedly, as though expecting to see someone behind him. "Something lives in that jamun tree," he said. "I felt it."

When Lal Khan grabbed his shoulders to steady him, he yelped.

"My arm!"

"Go get Haji Rahmat," Lal Khan said to Nisar. He walked the tree cutter over to the charpoy, sat him down, and covered his shoulders with a blanket.

"Calm down," Lal Khan said. "Think about what you're saying."

Nisar came running with Haji Rahmat close behind.

"This man says he was pushed off a tree," Lal Khan said to Haji Rahmat. "His arm seems hurt."

"I was pushed," the tree cutter repeated, as though convincing himself. His eyes darted about wildly in his sockets. "I was pushed. I was pushed."

"Okay, okay," Haji Rahmat said, as he sat down next to him. "Take a breath. Nisar, get him some water."

Nisar handed him a steel cup filled with water. The tree cutter held it to his mouth with his left hand and took a sip. Droplets trickled down his chin and neck.

"Are you in pain?" Haji Rahmat asked him. Then he said to Nisar, "Help him to the car. Let's get him to the hospital." As Nisar helped him up, and they made their way to the car, Haji Rahmat asked, "What I don't understand is how you fell."

"Sir, believe me, I was pushed," the tree cutter began. "I was up there in the jamun tree, working, and I felt someone was watching me. I saw no one, but I heard some ruffling. I thought it must be a cat or a bird," he took a deep breath before continuing. "The next thing I knew, something grabbed me by the back of my shirt and threw me off the tree. I was so taken aback, and the force of the push was so strong, that I couldn't hold on to the branches, and before I knew it, I landed on the ground. I was so scared, I couldn't even turn back to look, I just ran for my life!"

Nisar and Lal Khan helped the tree cutter into the car. Haji Rahmat sighed and gave the driver some money and instructions.

"Call me from the hospital when the doctor gives a diagnosis," he said to the tree cutter. "I will take care of the expenses."

As the car drove down the driveway out of the gates, Haji Rahmat and Nisar walked to the back of the house. They inspected the ground and the garden. Everything was still. The trees stood silent.

"Do you see anything?" Haji Rahmat asked.

"No, not really," Nisar said. "No one. Nothing. Maybe he is crazy?"

A few robins chirped from the treetops.

"Odd," Haji Rahmat said. "He's worked at the neighbor's house before. They told me he did an excellent job there."

Nisar brought a rake to gather up the debris that had been left behind, and I wondered what to make of this. Was the tree cutter crazy, or were we, for not believing him?

***

Zainab heard the story of the tree cutter from Nisar and Junaid, with flourishes from Jameela, who heartily agreed it was the presence of a jinn. You could never be too careful, she said, and shared stories of jinn taking over people's bodies, influencing their decisions and causing havoc. Zainab wondered aloud if Nadia had been playing by the trees yesterday; perhaps that's why she got sick? That evening, after dinner as Zainab and Haji Rahmat got ready for bed; she shared her concerns with her husband.

"Don't you find it odd," she began. "This is the second time there has been suspicion of a jinn in our house." She sat at her dressing table in her dressing gown and combed the tangles out of her hair. Haji Rahmat was already in bed, reading. He did not answer.

"I'm really worried about what happened with the tree cutter yesterday," she persisted.

Haji Rahmat glanced up from his book. "He has a minor fracture. I told you. I covered his wages for a month."

"Okay, but I am worried about the other part—the fact that he said he was pushed off the tree?"

"Nobody pushed him, Zainab. He was probably sleepy. Or drunk."

"You don't think it was a jinn?"

"Zainab, dear, you know how I feel about this."

"I'm worried. What if the reason Nadia is sick is because of the jinn? She always plays in the backyard, by the trees, even though I've asked her not to."

"My dear. Why should the jinn come attack her, or take her over, or whatever it is you think it has done? Why should it do that now, suddenly, after all these years?"

"I don't know why or how. All I know, is that there is too much of a coincidence in timing. She gets sick, and the next morning the tree cutter swears a jinn has pushed him off a tree."

"Stop being ridiculous. She has a stomach flu. Give her a few days, she will be alright."

Zainab poured a few drops of coconut oil in the palm of her hand, rubbed her hands together, and moistened the dry ends of her hair.

Haji Rahmat sighed. "Oh, please tell Nisar, the plumber will be here tomorrow to fix the piping under the kitchen sink. He came today to take a look, and the damage appears to be rather far-reaching."

"Something is not right," Zainab said. "I can feel it." She finished oiling her hair and piled it atop her hair in a bun, deep in thought while Haji Rahmat drifted into sleep.

***

A week later, when Nadia's health did not improve, Haji Rahmat called in a specialist. We ruled out diarrhea and dysentery because her stool was fine. When the fever went away and there were no signs of a cold, influenza was ruled out, too. Haji Rahmat sent for expensive vitamins and supplements from abroad to boost her immune system, but they didn't seem to help.

"She isn't any better," Zainab told the doctor. Jameela insisted it was tapeworms, and we had to hear the graphic and disturbing story of her nephew's struggle with tapeworms. The doctor ruled it out. Jameela was disappointed.

"Doctor. Sir, you must search properly. My nephew in Quetta had one pulled out of him."

"I'm a hundred and ten percent sure," he said, addressing Zainab, "that there are no tapeworms."

"Then it must be black magic," Jameela said confidently. "Someone has done black magic on our shahzadi. Doctor, perhaps this is beyond your expertise. Please do refer us to a different doctor, someone with a little more understanding of black magic."

The specialist, who had received his medical degree from Harvard University in the United States, stared down his nose at Jameela. "I don't have black magic referrals. Perhaps you can find one in your village." He sat at the foot of the bed and faced Nadia. "You must try to eat healthy food and go outside to play every day." Nadia did not answer him but picked at her nails.

When he left, Jameela sulked. "Today's doctors are like this only. Full of fluff. No one listens to us. Just because we aren't big shots, we have no influence."

"Jameela, it's not like that," Zainab pacified her. "You embarrassed him when you suggested he didn't know what he was talking about."

Jameela huffed. "He can't diagnose Nadia. What is his purpose? What kind of specialist is he?"

Zainab was befuddled herself. "I don't know. He's ordered some blood tests so let's see what those say," she said. "Please bring Nadia her milk, and some food. It's time for her vitamins."

Jameela headed into the kitchen, where she shared her irritation with the cook. "Harvard, shmarvard. The doctor turned out to be a fool. Couldn't diagnose anything. This is the problem with modernity." Jameela said. "Zainab and Haji Rahmat are just too modern. There is no other explanation. Nadia has obviously been affected by a jinn, or else its nazr."

Khansama sighed and began humming a somber melody. He placed a large black pan on the grate and lit a flame under it. When the pan began to sizzle with droplets of ghee, he flattened a ball of dough onto the pan, his fingers accustomed to the heat that emanated from the fire. The ghee hissed as it cooked the paratha to a golden brown, and the kitchen was filled with the comforting scent of ghee and flour. Jameela stirred turmeric and honey into a cup of milk and took a tray of food to Nadia's room.

The Calpol made Nadia drowsy, and she drifted into a fitful sleep. Zainab massaged her head and covered her feet with a blanket. Haji Rahmat kissed his daughter on the forehead and turned off the bedside lamp.

"You'll be well in no time," he whispered in her ear and squeezed her hand. Then they tiptoed outside her room, leaving her to sleep.

A week later, as suddenly as it had deteriorated, Nadia's health turned around. The color came back in her cheeks, she was happy to go out and play, and began bossing Nisar around as usual insisting he finish his reading lessons. Jameela attributed the recovery to prayer, Haji Rahmat to the new vitamins, and Khansama swore it was the paratha with ghee that had made her better. But I knew the real reason. A few days ago, Nadia heard Haji Rahmat and Zainab discuss how Aunty and Uncle Jee were leaving for Dhaka where they would be spending the next year to oversee the set up of a new jute factory.

16

It has been two months since Haji Rahmat's funeral and things are falling apart. The outdoor washbasins are grimy, and the drains are clogged. The gardener is shirking his duties. Normally Haji Rahmat would have kept him on his toes but now that he is no more, the oleander bush has overgrown and is infringing on the other plants. Zainab is overwhelmed with the influx of visitors and the additional responsibilities that have descended on her. These days, with so many visitors, who has time to keep up with the gardener's issues and tend to wilting flowers anyway?

It is not quite dawn. Soon sunlight will flood the rooms with warmth, but for now, the dew is still damp, glistening on blades of grass and the windshield of the cars like diamonds. The air, still cool, gently rifles through the plants, caressing the champa and the red flowerbeds of the Chinese honeysuckle. Nadia is awake in the kitchen, barefoot; her shawl wrapped tightly around her, and her cropped hair close on the nape of her neck. She calls out for Khansama. The noise alerts Junaid.

"Nadia," her brother says, striding into the kitchen. "You're awake. Good to see you. How are you feeling?"

Nadia turns, startled. But the sight of her brother relaxes her face.

"I have such a bad headache. I can't find Khansama. Will you go outside and call him in, please? Ask him to make me chai?"

She pauses for a moment and squeezes her eyes tightly shut; her fingertips pressed to her forehead. I notice her fingernails have been gnawed all the way back so the hyponychium is visible and raw.

"Wait, wait. I am so silly. Khansama went to see his family, right? Because of the cyclone in East Pakistan. I remember now. Has he returned?"

Junaid inhales sharply and bites his lower lip.

"Nadia. Nisar cooks for us now." He studies his sister's face. Then he says softly, "Khansama didn't come back."

For a moment, Nadia's mouth is an "o", and her eyes dark with confusion, as if she has been dropped in the middle of a new world. Before long, recognition registers on her face, and she smiles. "Oh, silly me. Nisar will make me chai, then." She rings the bell to call for Nisar.

Junaid turns away from her and reaches for the milk; the light inside the refrigerator illuminates his face. This is not the first time Nadia has had a memory lapse, and I can see her brother is upset, that he is trying not to cry. It has been twelve years since Khansama left us. East Pakistan is now Bangladesh.

17

1970

We should have known things would change when Khansama left, and that it would be the beginning of horrific things to come. We had heard that a cyclone had erupted from the delta of the Ganga and the Brahmaputra, and the storm surge engulfed the low-lying coastal areas in East Pakistan. Nearly overnight, entire communities and villages were washed away. Khansama's family, who lived in a coastal town in East Pakistan, hadn't been heard from, and in a panic, he hastily threw together his belongings, intent on rushing away to save what and whom he could. Haji Rahmat had tried his best to convince him to stay.

"There is no news of them," Khansama said. "What is the point of being alive, when I know nothing of my family?"

"You must return," Haji Rahmat said to him when he left. "God willing your wife and children are safe. Come back, bring them here."

Khansama promised he would return—but promises are hard to keep in times of disaster.

***

Two weeks passed and we heard nothing from Khansama. We had very limited knowledge of what was happening in East Pakistan, except what little we heard on the radio; our government kept broadcasting over the radio that relief efforts were underway, and things were under control. We worried about Khansama and his family, and Zainab was full of regret. "Poor Khansama," she said, "is there nothing we can do to help him?"

In early December 1970, Uncle Jee and Aunty Rabab returned from Dhaka unexpectedly. They came in the evening, after dinner, safe and sound from an area ravaged by catastrophe. The winter afternoon became more despondent than usual.

"When did you arrive?" Haji Rahmat asked.

"Yesterday. We flew in from Dhaka."

"What about the factories in Chittagong?"

"We couldn't make it there. Chittagong airport is under water."

"Really? Yahya Khan said he surveyed the disaster areas and things are under control?"

"We are not being given the whole picture. This is devastation like no other."

"But Radio Pakistan has been announcing so many relief efforts." Haji Rahmat went up to the television and switched it on to see if there were any news updates.

"That may be," Aunty Rabab said, "but information is severely limited. And supplies are not coming fast enough. In Tazmuddin, half the population is presumed dead."

Zainab clasped her hand over her mouth. "Oh God! That's where Khansama's family is. We haven't heard from him."

I thought of Khansama's merry smile and the way he sang old love songs while cooking. *My wife can hear me all the way in Tazmuddin, that's why I sing aloud,* he used to say.

"God help us." Haji Rahmat said. "The news is not showing anything right now." He turned off the television and began tinkering with the knobs on the radio. "Let's see if BBC is on. What about the factories?"

"The manager is there. But as you can imagine they are not operating at full capacity. They will probably be shut down for a while."

"You're not going back, are you? You shouldn't. Not till things are better."

"How are Nadia and Junaid?" Aunty Rabab asked.

Zainab glanced at the silver watch on her wrist. "They are probably getting ready to sleep."

Nadia was upstairs in her room, in pajamas. Jameela had just oiled the child's hair and tucked her into bed when she heard Zainab call for her.

"Okay, now off to bed. Your ammi is calling me, we have some guests downstairs." Jameela left the room.

As soon as Jameela was out of sight, Nadia jumped out of bed and tiptoed to her door. She opened the door a crack, and listened. She opened her door a crack to listen. Her mother was giving Jameela instructions.

"Please put some water to boil for tea for the guests," she said. "And bring some biscuits, the cake rusks. Oh, and if the children are awake, send them down, please. Uncle Jee and Aunty Rabab are here, they want to see them."

On any other day, Nadia would have been delighted to have an excuse to extend her bedtime and eat biscuits with guests. But now her eyes filled with anxiety, her face turned ashen, and her hands began to tremble. She returned quickly to her bed, lay down, and covered herself with a blanket. As she heard Jameela's footsteps come up the stairs, Nadia shut her eyes tight, pretending to be asleep.

"Nadia, your ammi wants you," Jameela called out. But seeing Nadia in bed, not moving, Jameela lowered her voice. "Oh, bless me, the shahzadi is asleep." She smiled, and smoothed the blanket over Nadia, tucking it around her feet. She turned the lights off and softly shut Nadia's bedroom door behind her.

"Nadia fell asleep already," Jameela told Zainab, who was pleasantly surprised that Nadia was becoming independent and respecting her bedtime without a thousand requests and fusses.

When Jameela left the room, Nadia once again crept out of bed, put her ear to the door, and listened. Sounds of conversation floated up the staircase from the family room downstairs. The television was on, broadcasting the nine o'clock news. Junaid was talking to Uncle Jee and Aunty Rabab. Nadia gnawed at her nails and listened. Then she locked her bedroom door and climbed back into bed.

With Uncle Jee having returned, I worried incessantly for Nadia. I began to see a pattern—some nights she had trouble falling asleep, and often, she would wake up with a start, as though from a nightmare. If her parents were with a guest in the drawing room, she obsessively asked Jameela who was over, or if anyone else was coming. The day after Uncle Jee's return, Zainab found Nadia hiding inside the wooden wardrobe in her bedroom. She scolded her daughter, and said that was not okay, hiding in cupboards could cause suffocation. She had the carpenter remove the lock from the cupboard so that it wouldn't shut properly. When Jameela cleaned out Nadia's toys and asked her where her favorite red Barbie doll was, Nadia mumbled that she didn't know. Jameela shook her head in disappointment and told her that she was a big girl and must take better care of her toys. But nobody put things together, nobody seemed to understand or pay too much attention as to why Nadia was behaving the way she did. Perhaps everyone was too overwhelmed by the events in East Pakistan, and so Nadia's behavior, even if it was noticed, was attributed to childhood whimsies.

18

1970-1971

The waters of the delta had not yet receded when President Yahya Khan held general elections in December 1970. The newspapers exploded with the results—the Awami League headed by Sheikh Mujeeb-ur-Rahman, a Bengali politician, had won by a landslide in the National Assembly. However, neither our army nor the most prominent party in West Pakistan, the Pakistan People's Party, was happy with this result. Trouble brewed between the two parts of the country, politicians were letting their egos get in the way and, of course, we were all going to suffer.

A few days later, as Haji Rahmat returned from his morning walk, he ran into Javed, his neighbor. Javed was dressed in a clean, starched kurta and shalwar, but his eyes appeared bloodshot and his face was uncharacteristically unshaven.

"Haji Rahmat, I'm leaving for Dhaka. Pray for my safe return. They have taken over our oil factory, and I must ... I have to do something."

Haji Rahmat's face betrayed worry. "Javed, this is not the time to go."

"We will lose our livelihood if I wait any longer."

"Better than losing your life. What does your mother say?"

"Mother is against it. But she is old. She doesn't know. I will be back in three days. I know a man who has a safe passage there and back. You should come, Haji Rahmat. Your new factory will be gone. It will be a pity."

The possible loss of his newest business venture weighed heavily on Haji Rahmat's mind. Just the other day, he had talked with Zainab about the unrest in Dhaka, and the risk of the match factory being taken over by rebel troops. Though he had considered going, Zainab's opinion had been a firm and irrevocable no. She often gave in to Haji Rahmat's whims but in this instance, she was resolute. He knew she was right, and he was optimistic that this mess would not last, that things would settle down, and then there would be time to go back and revitalize the factory.

The cab driver took the last few puffs of his cigarette, tossed the butt to the side, and extinguished it with his shoe. He banged the trunk shut and started the car. The engine gagged and spluttered.

"No, Javed, I am not going," Haji Rahmat said leaning into the window of the backseat. "There is no one to watch the businesses here if I leave. Junaid is still young."

"Then what?"

"I will wait it out. Wait till things settle and then I will go do what needs to be done. You should wait too, Javed. They are all mad, up in arms. Brothers divided."

Javed paused for a moment. He pointed his hands upward, to the sky, in a gesture of prayer, and then shook Haji Rahmat's hand.

"Please ask Aunty Zainab to check on my mother while I'm gone. And pray for me. I know you've always looked out for me."

Haji Rahmat's gaze followed the taxi as it receded down the block and made a right onto the main road. He pursed his lips and shook his head, like one mourning a loss, and made his way through the open front gate.

***

The next day we heard that Uncle Jee was leaving for East Pakistan, too. Haji Rahmat was on the phone with him, trying to persuade him to stay back and wait, but Uncle Jee said he knew people, and he would be able to get there and get back safely.

"Zainab, let's go," Haji Rahmat said to his wife. "Uncle Jee will be leaving shortly, we must see him before he leaves for the airport."

Zainab gathered her bag and dupatta, gave a few last-minute orders to Jameela, and called out to the children. But Nadia wasn't ready. She sat on the sofa cross-legged, reading a book.

"I don't want to go to their house," she complained. "I have to finish this book by tomorrow."

"Nadia come on, we will be back soon," Zainab said. "We must go see him before he leaves."

"Their house is so far."

"It's only fifteen minutes by car, dear."

"Can't I stay back with Jameela? Please."

Zainab thought to argue with her daughter but since Haji Rahmat was already in the car with Junaid, she gave in. "Nadia, you're getting to be very stubborn. I don't like this," Zainab said and walked out the front door.

Jameela eyed Nadia suspiciously. As Nadia read her book, Jameela oiled her hair, and braided it neatly into two braids she piled high on her head to keep the oil from getting on her face.

"Why didn't you want to go, Nadia?" Jameela asked. "Your ammi was annoyed with you."

"I don't like to go, Jameela. My stomach is hurting. And Aunty always forces me to eat samosas."

"*Eat samosas?* Since when is that a problem? I've seen you eat six samosas at one sitting without any complaints."

Nadia was silent.

"Uncle Jee would've liked to see you before he leaves. He is so fond of you. Always brings you gifts."

I watched as Nadia considered her words carefully. "Do you think a person is nice because he brings presents?"

"Usually."

"Don't you think that sometimes he is mean? Like, one day he yelled at Nisar."

"I'm sure Nisar did something to deserve it. He can be a real rascal."

Nadia dropped her head, staring down at her book. "Am I a rascal sometimes?"

"No, you're not a rascal."

A few minutes later, Jameela continued. "Anyway, why are you asking me this, Nadia? Was Uncle Jee mean to you?"

I could feel the air in my walls come to a standstill. Nadia chewed on her fingernail. "Is it important to keep a secret?" she asked.

"Yes, it is. Especially if you promised."

Without looking up, Nadia closed her book. Her face was shuttered. "Jameela, my stomach hurts. Can you please make me some mint water?"

"Of course," Jameela said and wandered off, without a backward glance.

And so, the afternoon ended at that, with an unfinished conversation, a stomach ache, and mint water.

***

I wondered if Jameela's conversation with Nadia had raised any suspicions in her mind, but I doubted it. It was difficult to be suspicious of Uncle Jee. He was a wealthy man who donated money to many causes and was extremely well respected in the community. Additionally, he was practically family and an investor in Haji Rahmat's business.

The more days that passed after Uncle Jee left for Dhaka, the more cheerful and happier Nadia seemed, small smiles creasing her lips more often than not. The recurring stomach aches that Nadia used to have subsided considerably, and once again she seemed relaxed, like her usual self.

One quiet afternoon, while Jameela hemmed Nadia's kurta, the conversation drifted to East Pakistan. Nadia's friend Mariam was over, and the girls were sitting with Zainab, cross-legged on either side of a substantial sixteen-by-twenty poster, working on a school project. Glue, magazine clippings, and markers were scattered around them. Jameela was sizing the hem of Nadia's school uniform kurta with pins.

"Jameela, before you stitch it, hold it up against Nadia, please, " Zainab said. "I want to make sure it's the right length."

Nadia stood up next to Jameela, who held the kurta up against her.

Zainab looked up at her daughter. "You're getting tall, beta." She smiled. "I think soon you will be taller than me." To Jameela she said, "Take it down, an inch and a half. It's looking too short."

Nadia held the kurta up against herself and faced Mariam. "Don't you think this is too long?" she asked her friend. "It looks so silly."

Mariam grimaces. "Aunty Zainab, Nadia is right, it looks like an old woman's dress."

"Ammi, see."

"Ufh. You girls are so silly." Zainab said. "It doesn't look proper to wear these kinds of short shirts to school. Jameela, keep it long. She'll grow again next month and then it will be a waste."

Nadia folded the hem up two inches. "No, do it this way. Don't listen to Ammi, Jameela. She is too old-fashioned!"

"Nadia. No arguing."

When her mother's back was turned, Nadia gestured to Jameela to make it shorter and put her finger to her lips to imply the need for secrecy. Mariam clapped her hand over her mouth to stifle a laugh, and Jameela shook her head and smiled. She undid the silver pins, folded the hem up a little more, and marked it with chalk. Then she threaded her needle and began sewing. It was quiet for a few minutes, while the girls applied glue on the backs of photographs and stuck them onto the poster. Then Jameela spoke.

"Baji, it's been quite a few weeks since Uncle Jee left. Have you heard from him? Or from Khansama? Or Javed?"

Nadia's face took on a pallid, jaundiced hue.

Zainab replied, "No word at all. Nothing. Aunty Rabab is getting worried. I hope Khansama is with his family. Javed—no one has heard from him in a month."

Jameela shook her head sadly.

Nadia gripped her marker tightly and colored with renewed intensity the border pattern she was working on.

Jameela continued. "What about Uncle Jee?" she said to Zainab. "Has anyone heard from Uncle Jee?"

"Nadia, beta," Zainab said. "Put some more glue here." Nadia, her fingers suddenly stiff and clumsy, reached for the glue bottle but her hand jerked, and she knocked it over.

Mariam stared intently at her friend. "Are you alright?" she asked. Nadia nodded without looking up and frantically grabbed a wad of paper napkins to wipe up the glue.

Zainab answered sadly. "No, we haven't heard from him. Rabab last got a phone call from him two weeks ago."

Nadia's eyes remained hidden, downcast. She said softly, "Ammi, do you think Uncle Jee will return?"

"We hope so," her mother responded.

"How do we find out?" Nadia pressed on, her voice a whisper.

Mariam looked up at her friend's pale face. "Don't worry Nadia. You worry so much."

"It's hard to know, beta," Zainab continued. "We should say a prayer for him, ask God to keep him safe. I think he is planning to stay there for a while, at least till things are under control. He has a lot of business there, a lot at stake."

If Zainab had been looking up at her daughter, she would've seen the relief on Nadia's face, and she would have thought it odd, that instead of being sad, as one should be upon hearing that a friend or family member was missing, her daughter radiated relief. Then she may have probed further, and maybe then, Nadia would have said something. But she was preoccupied with the hem of her daughter's kurta, and with glue on corners of pictures, so nothing of that sort happened.

"Make the stitches small and neat," Zainab reminded Jameela. "And let's make a dua for everyone; Javed, Khansama, and Uncle Jee."

Everyone in the room buried their faces in the palms of their hands and said a silent prayer. But Nadia did not pray.

***

It had been a few months since Javed and Uncle Jee had left, and we feared the worst. Had they been imprisoned? Or killed? And what was worse?

Mrs. Khalid, Javed's old mother, sat all day in her folding chair by the neighboring front gate praying on her tasbih saying, *my son is returning today, for sure he will return today.* And every evening when the sun would set, and darkness was beginning to settle in, the servants would ask her to come in the house. She would refuse and make a fuss, and scream and ask for her son.

Tensions had been mounting since India had entered the war and sided with East Pakistan. The West Pakistan military had launched preemptive airstrikes against India to show military prowess and now we waited for the retaliation, which was undoubtedly on its way.

As a means of protection, Haji Rahmat had prayers printed on sticker papers and had them distributed in the neighborhood; every home and car had on their door little white stickers with a prayer for peace and victory.

The morning's newspaper lay on the coffee table. "WAR TILL VICTORY," the headlines announced, as well as informing us that, "China promises help to Pakistan." Haji Rahmat sat on the curved green sectional in the living room, turning the knobs to get a static-free feed from the radio. The CEO of a prominent bank made an appeal to the people, asking for contributions to our National Defense Fund. Then Madam Noor Jahan came on the radio, her soulful voice saluting our brave soldiers on the front lines. When she sang, even those of us in our homes, away from the front lines, were so overwhelmed with patriotism that tears flowed freely, and we believed we would win.

We had heard that air raids were imminent. Zainab and Jameela spent the day covering all the windowpanes with black paper so no inside light would be visible from the outside at night. The Indian planes would only bomb places visible at night, and if the houses were dark, we would be safe. Nadia took the scraps of leftover paper and cut out doll chains.

At night, we vacillated between fitful sleep and insomnia, wondering when the siren would sound, alerting us that an air raid was about to begin.

Early in the morning, before the muezzin called the Fajr prayer, we heard it. Loud and inevitable, the siren wailed like a woman who had lost her child. It cut through the morning sky and penetrated our beings. Now it would be over. I wondered what would happen to us, to me, after the bombs fell.

Haji Rahmat jumped out of bed and went to find Lal Khan. "Blackout siren. Blackout siren. Turn off the lights, turn off the lights," he whispered.

The family huddled together. Nadia was awake; Junaid stirred for a moment and yelled, "blackout siren" in his sleep. Zainab wrapped her arms and a thick blanket around her children. The siren died down and we waited for the end.

"What will happen now?" Nadia asked. "At school, a teacher told me we are going to be finished. The Indian army is so much stronger than ours."

Haji Rahmat scolded her, "Don't say that. Our army is number one. We will win, everything will go back to normal."

The next morning, we heard that a house about ten kilometers from our neighborhood had been bombed, and everyone was worried, but also curious. The house became a tourist attraction. Nadia begged Haji Rahmat to take them to see it, and even though he rarely said no to her, he refused. But the obstinate children made the driver take them after school secretly, without Haji Rahmat's permission.

It was then that ten kilometers began to feel a little too close, and even though Haji Rahmat said we would be fine, I grew exceedingly worried about our safety.

***

We lost the war of 1971 and with it half of our country. It was a miserable, embarrassing defeat. I felt sorrow for the people, known and unknown, who had been lost, abandoned, killed, and forgotten during this short war. Here in West Pakistan, or shall I say Pakistan, because that is what it was now called, there was a strange sort of denial about the loss. Some still called the lost territory East Pakistan, rather than by its new name, Bangladesh, as though using its old name would be enough to bring the two halves of the country together. While Bangladesh celebrated its liberation with Sheikh Mujeeb ur Rahman sworn in as her first prime minister, we refused to accept Bangladesh's status as a country.

"What else did they expect?" Haji Rahmat said to Lal Khan as he took his early morning walk. "If the older brother does not take care of the younger brother, the family breaks apart. This is what happened with our country."

Lal Khan retorted, "Sir. It was India, that snake. If they hadn't interfered, we would still be fine. They have always been against us."

There is non-stop celebrating in every Indian town and city today, that the eastern border is no longer a threat," Haji Rahmat said. "But in this case the fault is ours. Our government treated

East Pakistan as a stepchild. If we worked to take care of our brothers and keep our country together, India would have been powerless."

Truth be told, many people here in Karachi thought Bangladesh wouldn't survive for long. I wasn't surprised that the country had split. I was more surprised it had stayed together for twenty-something years. How did this land appropriation of 1947 sanctioned by the British make sense anyway? How could a country have been expected to survive this way, two halves separated by miles of hostile Indian territory, while still recovering from a mass migration and civil war? How long were those in East Pakistan expected to stay loyal to a government that discriminated against them at every turn, treating them like second class citizens? How could an army that was supposed to protect its people turn on them with such savagery? And how misguided were we, in West Pakistan, to allow the propaganda to blind us into believing that our brothers and sisters in the East were traitors? How could a country atone for sins like this?

A few days later, Lal Khan opened the kitchen door and called out to Nadia, who was watching Jameela make rotis for breakfast. "Please give these to your father," he said and handed Nadia a small stack of letters. "I forgot to give this to him when he was outside earlier." Nadia took the stack and fanned through the envelopes as she skipped along to find her father.

A worn-out envelope lay like a relic in between the electricity and water bills. The edges were frayed, and it looked like it had been opened and resealed multiple times. The return address had been stamped out, but the postage mark said Dhaka. Nadia stopped in her tracks and dropped the other letters. She examined the envelope, and turned it over trying to figure out who had sent it. Worry was scrawled over her face. Her first instinct, like mine, must have been anxiety. Was it from Uncle Jee? Her face flushed, she ran to find her father, leaving the rest of the letters scattered on the floor.

Haji Rahmat was in the library. "Abbu, look what I found in the new mail," she said and handed her father the letter. "Will you open it? Is it from Uncle Jee?"

Haji Rahmat, immediately alert, took the envelope.

"No, not from Uncle Jee. It is from Khansama," he said. Khansama had written that he had lost everything in the floods, but his wife and children were alive, and so he was grateful. The West Pakistan government was not helpful. They did not do much for anybody. He was trying to find a passage back for all of them. But the letter was dated January 1971, before the war broke out, and we didn't know what fate his family had met since then.

"So, nothing about Uncle Jee?" Nadia asked.

"No, nothing in here. Poor Khansama. I do hope he is safe," Haji Rahmat sighed.

Nadia took the envelope from her father and checked it herself just to make sure he hadn't missed anything.

***

In December 1971, Mr. Bhutto became the prime minister of our newly truncated republic. Although many blamed Mr. Bhutto for the defeat, he was a charismatic man and a shrewd politician, and slowly he began to rally support. Once Bhutto signed the Simla Agreement, and we recognized Bangladesh as an independent nation, Bangladesh and India began slowly releasing prisoners of war. They returned hollowed out men, armed with horrific stories of unspeakable torture at their captors' hands. They told stories of how men, West Pakistanis and East Pakistanis both, had treated their brothers worse than pigs. Of how West Pakistani citizens in East Pakistan were rounded up by the Mukhti Bahini, never to be heard of again. And of how our army, that should have protected its people, had carried out the systematic, merciless killing of civilians, the rape of women, and the inhumane treatment of orphaned children in East Pakistan. We didn't hear it through the media, but from the many first-hand accounts of prisoners who had narrowly escaped, some who had been set free, and others who had found their way back home months later through luck, chance, and the mercy and friendship of strangers.

Once again, our government had not been honest with us. But the truth comes out, little by little, as small droplets that slowly merge together, and with persistence gain intensity till they break through the floodgates, upsetting the status quo with a deafening roar.

Javed was not one of the prisoners returned, and neither was Uncle Jee. Men who did not return were to be presumed dead, but Aunty Rabab wouldn't accept it and refused to have his funeral without a body.

Haji Rahmat tried desperately to find out Javed and Uncle Jee's whereabouts. He called in favors and contacted government offices; even managed to obtain lists of Pakistani prisoners who had been moved from Dhaka to prison camps in Bihar after the surrender, but their names weren't on any of the lists. Could it be that they had never even made it to the end of the war? Maybe Uncle Jee had perished in some horrible way at the factories he went to save? Maybe he had been gunned down on the street by the Bengali Liberation forces. I felt some semblance of relief, even gratitude, and hoped his death had been full of suffering. Aunty Rabab was inconsolable. Nadia was nervous and edgy. Any time Aunty Rabab called, Nadia's ears perked up, and she found some excuse to hover by the telephone table in the living room, so she could listen in and piece together the phone conversation. After every phone call her mother had with Aunty Rabab, Nadia was persistent in her questions about Uncle Jee's whereabouts.

Nobody knew where Uncle Jee was, and whether he was alive or not. The grayness of this answer bothered Nadia, she wanted to know definitively. One afternoon, a month after the prisoners had been released, Nadia returned from school to see her mother sitting on the chair next to the telephone, in deep conversation with someone, twirling the cord with her fingers thoughtfully. She sat down on the sofa and stared at her mother's face, trying to read her facial expressions. Once Zainab had hung up, Nadia began with her questions.

"Was that Aunty? Is Uncle Jee back? Is he alive?" Nadia bit her fingernails, looking uneasy, almost guilty, as though afraid her mother would figure out how much she hoped Uncle Jee hadn't returned.

"Stop biting your nails. I'm going to put chili on them," Zainab said to her daughter. "No, we haven't heard from Uncle Jee yet, beta. It's hard for all of us. You must stop asking me this every day. If you want to be helpful, just pray for him."

Nadia exhaled and went up to her room. The relief she felt was palpable. With each week that passed, and Uncle Jee wasn't heard from, Nadia decompressed. She looked happier and more relieved, as though each day a little of the anxiety and worry that had been building inside her was released. Zainab noted it and mentioned it to Haji Rahmat.

"She seems better now, doesn't she?" Zainab mused. "I think she's found things to distract herself and has stopped thinking about Uncle Jee. She was getting really worried, obsessing about him; for a while, she was asking me every day if he had returned."

Haji Rahmat sighed. "The children suffer so much in war," he said. "Much as we try to shield them from reality."

19

1976

Nadia turned fifteen in 1976. The anxiety and illness that had plagued her seemed a thing of the past; but now, both Haji Rahmat and Zainab began to worry about her future. It was one of those undisputed and unwritten laws of our society that at sixteen a girl should be receiving multiple proposals of marriage and that before twenty she should settle on a well-to-do husband who would provide for her needs. And so, as Nadia began nearing 16, Zainab began to entertain recommendations from Nasreen Bai, a professional matchmaker who had made it her life's joy and mission to bring unmarried souls together in matrimony. Being Zainab's twice removed cousin, Nasreen Bai took a personal interest in Nadia and came by on a weekly basis with advice and potential offers of marriage. *Girls have an expiration date,* she would say, and urge Zainab to act before it was too late

Zainab knew that although what Nasreen Bai said sounded crude and old-fashioned, it was better to find Nadia a husband sooner rather than later. Thus, she began entertaining families who had expressed a keen interest in bringing an offer of marriage for her daughter.

The Jahangirs were the first family we hosted. They came for tea on a Sunday afternoon—Mr. Jahangir and Mrs. Jahangir and their only son, Babar. What the young man lacked in height, he made up in width, and wore a well-pressed grey suit and black oxfords so shiny you could see his chins reflected in them. A quick bit of strategy in the seating arrangements allowed Nadia and the boy to be seated around the game table together. A pair of amorous lovers in the idyllic gardens of a French tapestry looked upon the prospective couple. Mrs. Jahangir settled comfortably into the green Chesterfield sofa about two feet away, from where she could eavesdrop effectively whilst pretending to give the young suitors some semblance of privacy.

The elder men sat on the sofa on the other end of the room, by the glass coffee table. Haji Rahmat offered his guest tea and then helped himself to a cup. Mr. Jahangir smiled at Nadia; Mrs. Jahangir sipped the tea and nodded at her son. Zainab gestured discreetly to remind Nadia to sit up straight.

It was Haji Rahmat who broke the ice. "How is business?" he asked.

"Good, by the grace of God," Mr. Jahangir replied. "How about you? The mill is doing well, I hope?"

"Not really. Bhutto's nationalization has really demolished our profits."

"Maybe it's time to consider other options," Babar offered from his seat by the game table.

Haji Rahmat shook his head. "There is not much else I can do at this point. Let's see what happens. Bhutto is planning to speak with some heads of industry in the next month." He took a sip of tea and continued, "that might offer some relief."

A moment later Haji Rahmat once again addressed Babar, who had not yet managed to engage Nadia in conversation, "So young man," he inquired, "what is new with you? How is work? What are your plans?"

"My plan, sir, is to be number one," Babar responded with almost comical flourish.

Nadia glanced at her mother and offered a barely stifled grimace. Zainab shot daggers back at her daughter.

"Wonderful," Haji Rahmat said. "I like ambition."

Babar continued. "We supply one thousand pounds of chicken salad to Pakistan International Airlines—the most that one company supplies to the airline. This year we topped our own numbers. We are the number one food supplier in the country, and I intend to keep it that way."

Nadia studied the rose polish on her manicured fingernails as she tried to suppress a laugh.

Haji Rahmat nodded.

"My professor at Oxford always said I'd be the best at whatever I did. And I will be. The best at running my company and," he paused for emphasis, "if given the opportunity, I'll be the best at taking care of your daughter."

Mrs. Jahangir gleamed with pride. "Oh, this boy. So much ambition," she said, her eyes actually moist with tears. "We are blessed to have him." Then she turned to Zainab.

"You have a son too, right? How old is he?"

"Yes. Junaid, he is twenty-one. I'm sorry he could not join us. He had a prior engagement."

Nadia smiled, happy with the knowledge that her brother was not present for this meeting. Junaid had been teasing her incessantly since he heard a family was bringing a proposal, erupting into love songs whenever he passed her in the hallway, giving name recommendations for her future children at the dinner table. Nadia had forbidden him from being anywhere near the drawing room when the guests came. Haji Rahmat insisted that under no circumstances should Nadia be stressed out; it would not bode well for the meeting—so Junaid had been asked to relegate himself to the club to play tennis that afternoon.

Now in the drawing room, there was some more talk of this and that, and the Jahangir family stood to take their leave.

As the boy got to his feet, he spoke for the first time directly to Nadia.

"It has been a pleasure to meet you, Nadia. I hope we will see each other again soon."

After they left, Zainab asked Nadia what she thought. "He seemed like a nice, ambitious boy; don't you think?"

Nadia rolled her eyes at her mother. "I suppose so. But it's not like we had a conversation. And I don't want to marry anyone who gets that excited about chicken salad."

"Nadia! He was talking about sensible things that men need to know about—work and industry. What would you rather he do?"

"I don't know ... talk about interesting things? Maybe ask me a question?"

"He was being polite. If he asked you something, you would've said he was being nosy."

"No, I wouldn't have—"

"Well, you didn't talk to him either. You just sat there, mute."

"I didn't want to say anything inappropriate. You always tell me, if I don't have anything nice to say, I should stay quiet."

Zainab threw her hands up in the air and turned to her husband. "Talk to your daughter."

"Nadia, I thought he seemed intelligent." Haji Rahmat spoke gently. "He will be able to take care of you. I do think he needs to exercise a little, perhaps a brisk morning walk a few times a week? You could encourage him."

"Ammi, see? Abbu also thinks he is overweight. I mean, it would help if he was a little ... you know what I mean."

"A little what?"

"A little nicer to look at."

"Don't be so superficial!" Zainab said. "Is this how I've raised you? You can't have it all! He is wealthy, from a good family, and has an established business. And he studied at Oxford. Surely with all that, you can overlook a little extra weight?"

Zainab cleaned up the crumbs from the coffee table and piled the teacups on the tray. She called out to Nisar to pick up the dishes.

"Zainab, leave her. Beta, think about it overnight and tell me tomorrow," Haji Rahmat said.

Her mother smiled primly. "Just keep in mind that they are a well-established and wealthy family. And you're no goddess yourself, so don't be superficial."

Nadia's eyes widened in indignation. "Ammi, that is so horrid!"

"No need to get upset. You know what I mean—"

Nadia marched off to her bedroom leaving her parents in the drawing room with Nasreen Bai.

Junaid walked in just as his sister stomped off, tennis racket in hand and a towel draped around the nape of his neck. "How did it go?" he asked. "Are congratulations in order?" He looked around, but everyone was too preoccupied to answer him.

"Why would you bring up the fact that he needed exercise?" Zainab said angrily to her husband. "Have you lost your mind?"

"So what if she didn't like him?" Haji Rahmat responded. "There will be others."

"Proposals like this don't come around often," she huffed.

"What happened?" Junaid prodded cautiously.

Zainab looked up at her son. "Oh, you're back. Good. Please go and talk some sense into your sister. We met a wonderful family, but she's finding a thousand faults with the boy. And your father has been completely useless in convincing her to accept the proposal."

***

Junaid found his sister sulking in her bedroom. "How did it go?" he asked. "You turned him down already?"

Nadia glared at her brother.

"Why don't you give him a chance?" he questioned.

"Well, firstly, he talked about silly stuff. Secondly, he was really not good-looking."

Junaid shook his head and laughed.

"It's not funny," she shot back. "He was really excited about chicken salad. Anyway, why don't you get married before you advise me?"

"I will when I meet someone."

Nadia faced her brother squarely, an impish grin instantly replacing the annoyance on her face.

"Is that so?" she inquired. "Then who is that pretty girl whose photo you carry around in your wallet?"

Junaid colored, and instinctively put his hand to his pocket as though to protect his wallet from his sister. "What?"

"Who is she?"

"I don't know what you're talking about," he said and averted his gaze.

"I think you do. Look behind your driver's license." She burst out laughing to see her brother's face turn crimson.

Junaid glared at his sister. "Why are you snooping around in my wallet?"

"Oh please. I wasn't snooping. I needed twenty rupees yesterday. Your wallet was lying right there."

He sat down on the edge of the bed. "You're such a pain."

"Well, what's her name?"

"Rania."

"How did you meet her?"

"None of your business"

Nadia's eyes glittered and bore into her brother's face.

"Fine. At a wedding."

"Do you *love* her?" she asked.

Junaid combed his fingers through his hair, awkwardly.

"Well?"

Junaid blushed. "Shut up please."

"What is the big deal? You're allowed to love someone. Why

don't you just tell Ammi and Abbu? They will be so happy that at least one of their children is ready to get married."

"She's Parsi."

Nadia's eyes widened. "Oh."

They both sat in silence for a minute, and then she continued with a cheeky grin. "Ammi will be angrier with you than she is with me."

"When I complete the next big project at the factory, I'll tell Abbu. Hopefully, his pride will dull his disappointment. He may even agree."

Nadia chuckled. "Just tell him, Quaid-e-Azam married a Parsi lady too. You're just following his footsteps because he is your role model."

Junaid laughed in spite of himself.

"But tell me something yaar, what does she see in you?"

Junaid rolled his eyes, got up from the bed, and walked out of his sister's room. "When is your next suitor coming?"

***

Much to Zainab's disappointment and chagrin, Junaid had been no help in the matter, and Nadia's decision did not change overnight. When Nasreen Bai called the next day to get an update, Zainab had to decline.

"But the family really likes Nadia," Nasreen Bai protested. "They found her very lovely, pretty, and mild-mannered."

"Well, Nadia is not agreeing. I don't know what to tell you. But please, just be polite. Say the girl is nervous about being married since she is a bit young."

"Certainly, I'll take care of it. I don't want Nadia to be known as a picky girl."

Zainab offered a heavy sigh. "I wish she would listen to me, Nasreen Bai. But you know girls these days."

Zainab gave her daughter a cold shoulder for the next two days. A few weeks later, Babar got engaged to one of Zainab's cousin's daughters and the amount of jewelry gifted to the bride-to-be was obscene in its extravagance. Zainab strode around the house, picking up objects and slamming them back down, and snapping at anyone who crossed her path.

Haji Rahmat tried to pacify his wife. "It's fine, dear. He is not the only boy in the world. She is only fifteen. There will be others. She didn't like him, what is the big deal?"

"The big deal is that he would've been so good for her. I just wish she would listen to me."

20

1977

Things began to change very rapidly when, in 1977, Prime Minister Bhutto was imprisoned by his army general, a short man with a no-nonsense mustache. General Zia-ul-Haq believed God had bestowed upon him the responsibility of bringing our country into accordance with his brand of Islam, and he took this self-imposed obligation very seriously. Strict laws infiltrated our constitution: laws against music and dance, alcohol, theft, and adultery. Some were minor tweaks in our established laws; others were drastic changes to our way of life.

Bhutto had already started banning clubs a few years ago to appease the religious conservative party, but things had not changed too much. Musicians and orchestras from around the world still came to play and in the evenings the city glittered and came alive, with qawallis and open-air shows. Hotels continued to host Christmas and New Year's parties; clubs still held their soirees; whether one called them festive or distasteful depended on who was asked. But with Zia in power, the celebrations were systematically being forbidden and the venues restricted. Zia's police discovered the discreet disco on the fourteenth floor of The Best Western Plaza, and immediately it was pronounced unlawful and shut down.

Most of Bhutto's cabinet was under arrest. Anyone who protested or opposed Zia was arrested or flogged. Journalists who spoke out disappeared. Curfews were imposed. Raising the flag of Bhutto's political party, the PPP, was banned.

Our household cautiously watched what unfolded with Bhutto's imprisonment. The television and radio were always on during the early morning and late evening. Every day at the hours of eight a.m. and nine p.m., when news updates were aired, we stopped what we were doing and turned our attention to the television. What was next? Would a pardon be issued? Would General Zia hold elections?

On a national level, we were trying to understand the repercussions of a plethora of new laws. On a domestic level, however, we felt things were under control. Nisar's ability to concentrate on his chores had improved significantly. He was finally able to clean without direction, and could, when occasion demanded, make tea, rice, and roti. His skill level took the burden off Jameela considerably. He had, however, developed a new habit: partaking in protest. He truly believed in Bhutto's slogan that promised the people "roti, kapra, makan" (bread, clothing, shelter). So enamored was he by our patriotic and charismatic leader, that he did not care whether Bhutto had been able to fulfill his promise to the people or not. He pored over newspapers in his free time and moved Lal Khan's radio next to his charpoy, so he could stay abreast of any developments. Inside when the news came on the television, he stopped his chores and watched with us, offering impassioned commentary. He began to excuse himself regularly in the afternoon, and one day when he returned with a bloody nose it was obvious, he had been at a "Release Bhutto" protest. He hid in the quarters from Lal Khan, stuffed cotton up his nostrils, bandaged his bruised arm, and rolled the sleeve of his shirt down to conceal it.

"Tomorrow we will march to Bhutto's House twice," Nisar said to Lal Khan later that evening. "If Haji Sahib needs anything, please cover for me."

Lal Khan was angry. "Bhutto may die or live, Nisar, but he will not save your life, and he certainly will not help you get a new job if you get fired for slacking off. Your mother depends on your paycheck. I know where you got that bloody nose. Don't pretend you tripped and fell."

"I'm not slacking. I finish my work and then go," Nisar retaliated. "Here we are talking about the state of our country and you are concerned about my job. Think of it, Lal Khan, think of it! Poor Bhutto—betrayed by his most trusted general and then tried for murder!"

"Jameela says you forgot to bring the groceries again today. There was no yogurt for lunch."

A wave of crimson washed over Nisar.

"Yes, I thought so," Lal Khan said. "Have some consideration for your poor mother. What would she do without you? Go get fennel seed and mint and stay clear of the protests on the way to the market, unless you want your mother to have to bury her own son."

Loyalties are fickle in times of peace, but even more so in times of unrest. Bhutto had vacillated between being despised to being beloved. His popularity was at a low when Zia overthrew him, but the arrest had increased Bhutto's appeal six-fold. And now, the same people who had blamed him for our loss of East Pakistan were rallying behind him.

Junaid was working on finishing his BA at university and had started working with his father at the factory. He was worried about business, but Haji Rahmat would always say, *"We are fine, Pakistan will be fine."* That was the curious thing about Haji Rahmat. I couldn't figure if it was stubborn denial or impenetrable optimism.

"Why can't we all go?" Nadia asked Haji Rahmat after dinner when she heard Jameela complaining about Nisar sneaking out to a protest.

"It is too dangerous," he answered.

"But Junaid went!" she blurted out. "There was a protest at his university, and he was there."

"Junaid ... is that true?" Haji Rahmat asked, his voice on the verge of anger.

"Oh my God," Junaid said. "Nadia, you snitch. Abbu, she went too. There was a women's protest at her school started by Bhutto's daughter, and she joined in."

If the fact that Junaid had been at a protest upset Haji Rahmat, the knowledge that Nadia had been at one forced him on his feet, his eyeballs bulging out of their sockets.

"Is this true?"

Nadia colored and nodded. "I mean, it was just on campus. I didn't go on the streets."

"I need you to hear me loud and clear. I forbid you from joining any protests. If I hear of this again, you will be not allowed to go to school anymore. You cannot be at a protest!" He slammed his fist on the table. "You too, Junaid. The two of you do not understand how dangerous they are. What if you were kidnapped, or targeted? Zia's men are everywhere! Do you know what the punishment is for political activity? Public flogging ... and that is only the beginning."

The siblings stared down at the table. Junaid twisted his napkin, his lips tightly pressed together, but Nadia said, almost under her breath, "Abbu, we have to take a stand."

"Not this way. I cannot have you in danger. Your protest won't do anything that foreign government pressure can't do. There is immense pressure on Zia from the world over, especially our strongest allies. Jimmy Carter has asked for Bhutto's pardon, and so have Deng Xiaoping and King Khalid of Saudi Arabia," Haji Rahmat settled back into his chair and continued, "It is just a matter of time. Bhutto will be pardoned."

"But we can't sit back and do nothing. This is our country."

"You can help your country through social service. Go work at an orphanage or teach at a government school. Just stay away from protests and politics."

21

1979

On the fourth of April 1979, as the family ate breakfast, Haji Rahmat turned on the kitchen television set to catch the morning news update. The news anchor sat stiffly, his face nearly the same shade as his white shirt, as he relayed the headlines in a monotone:

This morning, at approximately two a.m., ousted Prime Minister Mohammed Zulfikar Ali Bhutto breathed his last. He was found guilty by the Supreme Court on charges of corruption and the murder of Mohammed Ahmad Khan Kasuri and was hanged at the Rawalpindi District Jail. His body has been flown for burial to his family. Bhutto's wife and his daughter Benazir Bhutto have been placed under house arrest."

The news reporter continued relating details without emotion, and images flashed on the television screen in rapid succession. The breakfast room fell still, frozen. That morning, as the family gathered around the dining table, it appeared that they may have been posing for a daguerreotype, and their images were fused forever in my memory. Haji Rahmat at the head of the table, holding a teaspoon, Zainab sat on his right with a half-eaten peach on her plate. Nadia stood behind her mother with a teacup in her hand. Junaid at Haji Rahmat's immediate left reaching for the eggs. All of them stared straight ahead, at the brown Hitachi television screen, breakfast forgotten.

Nadia finally spoke articulating each syllable slowly. "He hanged him! Are we in the bloody Middle Ages? Harami!"

Nisar was next to speak. He launched into a litany of abuses, and in tears, asked for the wrath of God to avenge Bhutto's death.

No one raised an eyebrow at the indelicate use of words. Haji Rahmat normally would not tolerate this language in his home, especially from his daughter, and never from Nisar, but today was not an ordinary day.

"God help us!" Jameela said and started reciting the Fateha prayer.

The television aired Zia-ul-Haq's comments on repeat. He sat in his military uniform on his chair, with the green and white flag placed in the backdrop in a show of patriotism, and spoke firmly, without regret:

"The Supreme Court has spoken, and we have given the people of Pakistan the rule of law."

But the hanging was anything but the rule of the law. It demoralized the nation, and we felt suspended in a limbo of fear and uncertainty. Condolences poured in from the world over, announced reporters. There were no elections. A referendum announced that Zia-ul-Haq would be president.

***

One would expect a revolt of great magnitude after such a hanging. One would think there would be yelling in the streets and a demand for justice. Instead, fear crept into our hearts, and a quiet took over, as if the city itself were holding its breath to see what was next. Most heads of Bhutto's political party were imprisoned. We adhered to strict curfews and avoided the repercussions of breaking new laws. Widespread fear created the illusion of calm.

There seemed no other choice except to settle into life, into our own distractions to deal with the turmoil. Nasreen Bai continued with marriage recommendations for Nadia and arranged for more potential suitors. On Tuesday we received a wealthy family from Lahore. Wednesday brought the Patels, who ran huge industries; Thursday evening brought with it the Abduls, who were associated with the military. Nadia rejected them all. By Thursday night Zainab was despondent and somber. On Friday, Nasreen Bai called with enthusiasm; she said she had found the perfect family, they were modern and wealthy, and the icing on the cake was that the boy was also known to be handsome.

Zainab was hopeful that maybe this boy would be the one. Although Nadia had turned down several other suitors, Zainab had still not completely recovered from Nadia's rejection of Babar, her first suitor.

"Wear your blue shirt," Zainab said to Nadia. "The one with the flowers. It makes you look pretty. I'll have Jameela iron it. Also, Nasreen Bai has said not to wear high heels, the boy is not very tall."

Nadia looked quizzically at her mother, "What do you mean?"

"I don't have specifications."

"So, if I were to marry him, I could never wear heels again?"

"That will be between you and him. But I need you to make a good first impression."

"Are you sure I should wear my blue kameez? What if he doesn't like blue?"

Zainab turned to answer and, realizing that Nadia was being cheeky, knit her dark eyebrows together in despair. "You're never going to find a husband with that attitude," she said primly and left Nadia to her own thoughts.

As evening drew to a close, Nisar and Jameela busied themselves in the kitchen preparing refreshments. At eight p.m., the doorbell rang, and our guests were shown to the drawing room. As they were seated, we noticed a key component missing.

"Your son, Mrs. Ahmed," Zainab inquired politely. "Is he running late?"

Mrs. Ahmed sat down and gestured to her daughter to join her on the couch.

"Oh, my son won't be joining us today. He had to travel for work."

An entire minute of silence passed in the room. Then, Nadia turned to Zainab with a tight-lipped smile and shook her head.

"Oh. I wish you had told us. We could've rescheduled," Zainab said.

"No need. We figured we may as well come, my daughter and I could meet your daughter, and we can relay the information to him."

Nobody responded.

"But don't worry. I figured you may want to see him, so I have a photograph here."

Before anyone had a chance to recover, Mrs. Ahmed fished out a manila envelope from her purse and handed over an unnecessarily large glossy photograph.

"They say he looks like Amitabh Bachan," she announced.

I analyzed the photograph to see similarities between the Indian movie star and Mrs. Ahmed's son. The boy was, I must admit, a nice looking fellow, clean-shaven and with a nice healthy head of well-styled dark brown hair. Since the photograph was cropped at the chest, the question of his height had still not been answered. He appeared pensive, uncomfortable, as though he knew his photo was doing the rounds in the drawing rooms of potential in-laws.

As the photo reached Nadia, she glanced at it dismissively and passed it on to Mrs. Ahmed, who was seated to her right. Mrs. Ahmed thrust the photo back onto Nadia's lap.

"Now, now, don't be shy, dear. Look at the photo properly. Isn't he charming?"

Before Nadia could speak, Zainab glowered; a warning for her daughter to remain quiet.

Mrs. Ahmed took the photograph of her son and held it up against Nadia. She ran her eyes up and down, making a detailed analysis.

"I think they make a most attractive couple," she said finally.

Mrs. Ahmed's daughter, who sat next to her mother, looked to and from Nadia and her brother's photo. The young woman laughed a silvery tinkling laugh and tossed her hair behind her head.

"They do, Mummy, they really do!"

When they finally left, the usual recounting of the meeting commenced.

"What do you think?" Nasreen Bai said.

Nadia scrunched her nose as though smelling something rank. "What do I think of what?" she asked.

"The boy, of course!"

"Nothing! He wasn't here. How am I to think anything of him? How do they show up without their son, Ammi? Am I a thing on display?"

"Stop being dramatic, Nadia."

"Why don't you leave me alone and find someone for Junaid instead?" she snapped. "He is older than me, he should get married first."

"Don't you worry, I have some girls in mind for him," Nasreen Bai answered, her voice joyful.

"Well, Nasreen Bai, I guarantee he won't like who you bring." Zainab raised her eyebrows at her daughter, "are you trying to tell me something?"

Nadia sighed and shook her head no.

"Then don't change the subject," she said to her daughter. "Junaid will get married when he is ready. He needs to focus on the factory now."

"Double standards," Nadia muttered under her breath.

Zainab glared at her daughter and then turned to Nasreen Bai. "This was a disappointing meeting. How can we move forward without meeting the boy?"

"You know how people are, Zainab," Nasreen Bai said. "Sometimes they like to make sure the girl is *worth* showing to their son. But I agree. This was not a good use of our time. And here we had prepared kheer and samosas to feed an army! What a waste."

Several weeks passed before Nasreen Bai arranged another visit. This was not to say that she had given up, rather she was busy screening the next slew of suitors, so there would not be any more disappointments. She called Zainab with updates and recommendations twice a week.

22

1980

General Zia-ul-Haq reckoned that curbing the arts and music would be a good strategy to curb resistance, and he was rather clever about it. He restricted activities that hampered the cultural correctness he was imposing, while celebrating those that propagated his vision of an Islamic state. Journalists who criticized him were publicly flogged, writers were imprisoned, and artists could be incarcerated for crimes such as stealing cyclostyle machines, if they were not careful. But as he did so, one of our most beloved pop stars emerged on the scene, and took not only our country, but the entire subcontinent by storm. Nazia Hasan, a fifteen-year-old Pakistani girl shot to stardom when she sang the vocals for "Aap Jaisa Koi", a song composed by the British-Indian music producer, Biddu. Her song was part of the soundtrack for the Indian movie, *Qurbani*.

Since Partition, with the exception of a few years, both India and Pakistan guarded their borders closely, hoping to prevent cultural osmosis between two regions whose people had been together longer than they had been apart. Since the war in 1965, the ban had been rejuvenated with gusto, and Indian movies were not easily available to us. But no matter–when our governments emphasized bans, our people found other ways. Neither Pakistanis nor Indians, though they may have disliked each other on some fronts, were going to let bans and politics get in the way of their entertainment. Grainy copies of Hindi films proliferated the market in Pakistan, available to rent for 20 rupees a day. And on the other side of the border, bans did little to prevent our Indian brethren from enjoying the latest Pakistani dramas, which were available courtesy of their local video rental stores.

A few months after *Qurbani* had been released, Nadia and Mariam came home from school with big smiles on their faces and rushed to the television. Nadia unzipped her school bag and pulled out a VHS tape, which she proceeded to pop into the VCR.

Zainab, who had just come in from the kitchen, spotted her daughter and her friend twittering excitedly.

"Hello girls, what is that you are you watching?" she inquired.

"Ammi, you won't believe it, we got a music video of Nazia Hassan singing 'Aap Jaisa Koi!'"

"Oh, where did you get that from?"

"My friend Rani's uncle lives in Birmingham, he brought it for her. I think it was recorded in England," Nadia gleamed. "Do you want to watch with us?"

Zainab settled into the velvet sofa while the girls sat cross legged on the ground right in front of the small brown television.

"She's a good girl, that Nazia Hasan," Zainab said. "I read an interview of hers. She has had some offers to act in films, but she is not interested; she wants to finish school first."

The recording began with a little static, but that didn't matter when Nazia Hassan began singing. Radiant in her red jumpsuit, her dark hair falling in waves over her shoulders, she swayed demurely on the stage as she sang, her voice and grace making it hard to believe that she was only fifteen.

"Ah she is so beautiful."

"And so proper and well mannered," Zainab said. "Even as she sings that song, she is not vulgar in any way."

"Her brother is really handsome too. His name is Zoheb."

Zainab's raised one eyebrow at her daughter and laughed. "That's why you don't like anyone Nasreen Bai brings? You're waiting for someone like Zoheb Hassan to come along."

Roses bloomed in Nadia's cheeks. "Stop it, Ammi," she said, and then added categorically, "he is younger than me. It would never work out."

As the song wrapped up and a stream of static ensued from the video, even the seat cushions on the Chesterfield deflated with disappointment. Mariam pressed the rewind button so they could watch it again. Finally, after watching it four times over, the girls walked over to the dining table to have lunch.

***

Meanwhile, Nasreen Bai had been successful in acquiring another possible suitor. The Khans arrived on a Sunday afternoon. Their son, the seventh suitor, was significantly taller than Nadia and had sharply chiseled features as though his jaw and cheekbones had been carved out of fine marble. Although he did not resemble Zoheb Hassan, he was handsome, so maybe there was hope.

The family settled into the usual seating arrangements. Nadia across from the boy, close enough to talk, but still a proper distance away. The boy's mother and Zainab sat on the couch across from them; and Haji Rahmat and the boy's father settled in the chairs to the left of their wives, the farthest away from the prospective couple.

It was quiet at first. Then the boy addressed Nadia.

"So ... tell me, what are your plans for the future?" he inquired.

Nadia smiled. "I'm studying at Karachi University."

"What do you plan to do there?"

"I'm not sure as yet, but they have a good department for political science and—"

"Are you planning to go into politics?" Mrs. Khan practically choked on her samosa and turned swiftly to face Nadia.

"Not exactly—" Nadia started but then stopped abruptly at a look from her mother.

Mrs. Khan took a minute to soothe her esophagus with a sip of water before she continued. "Then why study political science? Are you thinking about law? With running a household and raising kids, I doubt you will have time for a career in law or politics."

"I'm not going into politics," Nadia said. "It just seems like an interesting subject to study."

Mrs. Khan's shoulder relaxed, and her facial wrinkles smoothed out as if Nadia had been absolved of a crime. "Your greatest aspiration must be to look after your family. It's hard to balance a job with family life and being a politician. That would never work."

Haji Rahmat glanced at his daughter, who was biting her lip, and probably her tongue. "Well, Mrs. Khan. Our daughter is still young, so she does not have to choose between her education and raising children," he said. "She can certainly do both."

Nadia's jaw relaxed, and she smiled at her father in appreciation.

Mrs. Khan seemed to consider Haji Rahmat's comment. She opened her mouth to speak but Zainab interjected.

"Would you like something else to eat?" Zainab filled a plate with pastries and handed it to Mrs. Khan. "And what about you?" She turned to Mr. Khan. "What can I get for you?"

"Oh, please don't trouble yourself," Mr. Khan said graciously. "I'll help myself."

He got up to pour himself a cup of tea and then addressed Haji Rahmat.

"How is the factory doing these days?"

"Getting things back on track," Haji Rahmat replied. "Denationalization has helped and I think we are off to a good run."

Mr. Khan stirred sugar into his teacup and resumed his position on the couch. "Good to hear. So many changes these days. Makes you wonder what will happen. Especially with these new laws, Karachi has become a different city."

"Indeed. The whole atmosphere seems different. One day you're watching Dizzy Gillespie play sax with a snake charmer in the park, and next thing you know, all concerts in the city are banned." Haji Rahmat frowned.

Mr. Khan pondered. "Some of Zia's laws do seem a bit Draconian."

"Agreed. We've done without his laws for the past thirty or so years. No need for them now," Haji Rahmat pointed out.

"Haji, please. You don't need to keep saying this," Zainab twittered. "Even the walls have ears."

"I'm only saying what's true."

"But Haji Rahmat," Mrs. Khan said. "He's been saying he is just trying to make the laws Islamic."

"We know that's a ploy. Our laws were never un-Islamic to begin with. He is just doing it for political gain."

The boy interjected. "Well, things had deteriorated under Bhutto. We did need a change. Perhaps it could be a positive change?"

"If you ask me, his ordinances will cause more trouble than anything else. There is no check to his laws. There have already been pockets of protests."

"True," Zainab said. "I also read that he is trying to emphasize a change in dress for women; recommending modest clothing and head covering."

Mrs. Khan interjected hopefully. "Maybe there will be some good changes? He has made some sensible laws, too, like the compulsory paying of charity."

Haji Rahmat shook his head. "I don't know, it's a slippery slope."

"Maybe it is more talk than action. Maybe the laws won't stand." Zainab said.

Nadia had been quiet this entire time observing the guests. Now she spoke suddenly. "They're already standing, Ammi. Things are happening, and we can't do anything about it."

Mrs. Khan immediately glanced at Nadia with disapproval.

"Ah, I agree. Things look worrisome. Did you hear about that case with the housekeeper?" Mr. Khan said. "Bad situation, getting worse."

Mr. Khan was referring to the story that had been on the news, of a young blind housekeeper who had been raped by her landlord and his son. In outrage, the young girl's father had launched a complaint but since she was blind and could not identify her rapists, the men had gone free. However, she was in danger of being imprisoned on grounds of adultery. Of course, here in the drawing room, it was understood that everyone had the decency not to discuss the awful specifics of the case.

Nadia was immediately provoked by the mention of this topic.

"That is exactly what I mean," she said, "If a woman reports an incident or gets um, you know, *with child*," her voice dropped to an octave above a whisper when she said *with child*. Zainab glared at her daughter, who ignored her and went on. "The woman automatically implicates herself, but the man can go free. Zia's law doesn't do anything except hurt women." Nadia's voice wavered. "And even if she is absolved, the stigma is so severe that no one will ever let her forget it." Suddenly her shoulders drooped, as did her eyelids, as though putting these words together had taken everything out of her.

"There is still hope," Zainab said quickly. "The Women's Action Forum is working very hard on this case."

"It's always the girl who suffers," Nadia added softly, picking at her nails.

Zainab seared her daughter with a look, as though willing her to change the subject. "I am sure this will be resolved."

"And so what if it is? It still won't change what has already happened," Nadia said. "And for sure there will be more." Her eyes glistened with tears.

The boy looked at Nadia with empathy. "Are you alright?" he said and offered her a napkin, which she accepted. Zainab shifted in her chair and smoothed her hair; no doubt uncomfortable at the somber turn the conversation had taken.

There was a delicate clink as Mr. Khan set his empty teacup on the coffee table. "Intelligent daughter you got there, Haji Rahmat.

We all need to question the status quo. And stand up against inequality. That's the Islamic way. That's what Jinnah wanted for Pakistan." Mr. Khan paused for effect, pleased with his speech.

Zainab interjected. "Thank you, you are very kind, Mr. Khan."

I think the last thing she wanted was for this discussion to continue and for Nadia to comment more on the case or on Zia's new laws. She tried to end the discussion. "We have female members of parliament. They are strong intelligent women. They will put up a fight for sure. We are not going to be oppressed so easily. Anyway, enough talk of politics."

Mrs. Khan nodded vehemently in agreement.

"So," the boy said to Nadia. "Do you have other hobbies? Like embroidery or cooking? My sister said she took a cooking class from Mrs. Hussain. It changed her life."

Nadia smoothed the crinkles in her skirt and began to answer, but Mrs. Khan spoke up first.

"Yes, indeed. Those are excellent pursuits. Politics is not a field for young women. I would strongly advise against it. It does not behoove a young woman with so much going for her to throw it all way and waste her time in politics, because as you know—"

"Mrs. Khan, I am not going into politics!" Nadia snapped.

"Oh, dear!" Mrs. Khan sat back at the interruption, then laughed nervously. "I'm just saying it generally, based on your analysis of Zia's laws."

"Mrs. Khan, please try some mille feuille," Zainab interjected and served a slice of the delicious flaky concoction to her guest. "May I refresh your tea?"

Mrs. Khan pushed the pastry away. "Oh no, Zainab," she said. "I've had too much already!"

Nadia stared at the landscape painting that hung behind the Chesterfield sofa. Her eyes were glazed over and seemed to reflect the dull gray-green of the lake in the painting. Her mind was somewhere else now, no longer in the drawing room. "Please excuse me for a moment," she said, and without waiting for anyone's okay, she got up and left the room.

With every moment that passed, I could see Zainab growing more worried. Ten minutes later, her daughter had not returned, she excused herself on the pretext of getting more tea. She found Nadia sitting on her bed, her head bent low, cradled in her lap.

"Beta, what is the matter? We are sitting there, waiting for you to return. They are waiting to talk to you."

Nadia lifted her head slowly, as though she could not bear its weight; her face wore a withdrawn expression.

"I'm not feeling very good. I can't go back in there now."

Zainab sat at the foot of the bed. "This is why I don't like to discuss politics. Why in God's name would you work yourself up into a frenzy, debating women's rights during a meeting with a prospective suitor?"

"I … I just … " Nadia sighed. "I'm done meeting people Nasreen Bai brings. When I am ready, I will find someone myself."

Annoyance now flickered on Zainab's face. "I'm trying to be understanding, but frankly I don't understand what is the matter with you. There is no need to be so rebellious. Can you just be decent in front of them? You don't have to marry him, but can you just be proper? For my sake?"

"You don't understand anything, Ammi." Nadia whispered.

"There is a time and place for everything. And the time to theorize on Zia's ordinances is not when we are meeting suitors. The Khans don't make the laws! They're just here to find a wife for their son, not to discuss indelicate topics."

Her daughter's face fell. Zainab softened her tone.

"Beta, she said kindly. Please. Just come now. What will they say? That the girl abandoned them in the middle of the meeting?"

Nadia got up and followed her mother into the drawing room.

***

"Can I get anyone something else?" Zainab asked her guests, as she and Nadia re-entered the drawing room.

But the Khans were getting ready to leave.

"We have a dinner engagement, we need to head out," Mr. Khan said politely. "Thank you for a lovely evening."

The boy shook hands with Haji Rahmat and gave the women an appreciative smile. Nadia hardly offered more than a wave.

After the family left, Zainab said. "I already know your answer, but I urge you to think about it overnight. He is a nice boy, handsome and well-established. His mother was the feisty one, but you're not marrying her."

"Fine, I will think about it," Nadia said. She seemed to have no energy to engage with her mother.

The next morning, before Zainab had the opportunity to press her daughter for a decision, Nasreen Bai called. The Khans had decided to retract their proposal; they had found Nadia too *politically inclined* and *outspoken*, and while those were great qualities, they just wouldn't be compatible with their family. Zainab was horrified at the rejection. Nasreen Bai recommended that Zainab take some time to explain to her daughter the meaning of compromise, and the importance of being proper at meetings with potential families.

"I know, Nasreen Bai," Zainab said. "I just don't know what got into her yesterday. She's not usually this way."

***

But of course, Nasreen Bai couldn't keep away for long. Once she started something, she needed to see it to the end, and matchmaking throbbed in her veins like blood. A week later she dropped in for a visit as the family was sitting for breakfast.

"Salam, Nasreen Bai," Zainab said, stirring sugar in her cup of tea. "Didn't expect you over. Come please join us. What will you have?"

"Just some water, please."

Zainab nodded. "Of course. Tell me now, to what do we owe the pleasure of your company?"

Nasreen Bai smiled. "I have good news. Remember the Ahmeds? The mother called. They really liked Nadia, and they want their son to meet her."

"Aren't they the ones who came without their son?" Nadia asked. She added a shake of pepper to her omelette and took a forkful.

Nasreen Bai nodded. "Yes. But they are good people and a top-of-the-line family, too. They really want their son to meet you."

"They had their chance," Nadia said.

Nasreen Bai gave a tight-lipped smile. "Nadia, stop being difficult. Zainab listen to me; they are requesting another meeting. What do you say?"

Haji Rahmat dipped his roti in a tub of fresh cream and took a sip of chai, but said nothing.

"I think it is a great idea," Zainab said. "Nasreen Bai, please set a date."

"Ammi, the son did not have the decency to show up. He probably won't show up again. I don't want to meet them. I need a break from meeting boys, I have to focus on my exams."

Zainab glared at her daughter. "What shall I say to them? That our daughter has chosen to become a spinster?"

Nasreen Bai piped in. "What will all this studying, and a degree do for you, anyway? It won't make child labor any easier. I say bag the fellow now, and study later."

The nineteen-year-old grimaced.

Nisar came in with a glass of water and a cup of tea and set it on the placemat in front of Nasreen Bai.

"Maybe you can just meet them, give them a chance," Haji Rahmat said to his daughter softly. "It can't hurt."

Nadia shook her head no.

"For God's sake Nadia!" Zainab said. "My brother's daughter got married at sixteen. Met the first boy and agreed. And now she is pregnant with her second child. You will get a bad reputation in the community. You find fault with every boy. The Khans already turned you down. And there have been murmurs that you want to be a politician."

"Ammi, please—"

Zainab continued. "Look at our neighbor's daughter. She did the same thing, said no to every one, and then turned twenty-six and no one was interested in her anymore. Now she is thirty-two, lives at home, and takes care of her old mother, nothing more to live for. Haji, do you want Nadia to die alone?"

Haji Rahmat knew better than to say anything, so instead of engaging in conversation with his wife, he just cleared his throat.

"Oh, and remember Babar?" Zainab added. "I'll have you know that his wife is *thriving*. They have two children, and he took his wife for the delivery to St. Mary's hospital in London."

Nadia shrugged.

"And they travel exclusively in first class with their nanny." Nasreen Bai added with particular emphasis on the words *first-class* and *nanny*.

Haji Rahmat who had moved on from breakfast to reading his paper raised one unruly eyebrow at Nadia.

Zainab continued. "We should be grateful people are still interested in meeting you. What with the way you behaved at the last meeting with the Khans."

"Okay stop, Ammi, please, just calm down. I'll meet him." She threw her napkin on the table and left the room, breakfast unfinished.

"She will be the death of me, that girl. Haji, these are your genes, stubborn and independent."

"I think we should meet in a neutral place," Nasreen Bai said after a moment's consideration. "Maybe a coffee shop in a hotel."

"Why?" Haji Rahmat asked.

"Just to change the scene."

"Why does a scene need changing?"

"Well, Haji Rahmat, your wife has told me there is suspicion of a jinn in the house. To be honest, I think that is why Nadia doesn't agree to marry anyone. The jinn prevents it."

"That is ridiculous!" Haji Rahmat said. "Zainab, why do you indulge in these silly superstitions?"

"Just to be on the safe side, Haji."

Haji Rahmat shook his head and sighed. "As you wish, Zainab. If that makes you feel better, so be it."

***

Nadia met Mr. and Mrs. Ahmed's son for tea at a fancy coffee shop at the Intercontinental Hotel.

From what I gathered through the family discussion later that night, the meeting had gone unexpectedly well. The boy, his name was Tariq, was happy Nadia was enjoying her time at university. He didn't bring up cooking or embroidery. He also apologized for the photo incident and insisted that his mother had done it without his knowledge. They sat and talked for an hour while the mothers sat a stone's throw away at a separate table. Compared to the others, he seemed like a modern Renaissance man, or perhaps expectations were just so low at this point.

A few days later, when Nadia told her parents that she had decided to marry him, Zainab couldn't believe her ears.

"This is the answer to all my prayers," she sobbed and hugged her daughter.

Nasreen Bai came with garlands of flowers and even Zainab's mother, who was bedridden, came over to rejoice. Nasreen Bai considered it a personal victory. "I knew meeting elsewhere was a good idea, look how quickly she agreed!"

I felt miffed. How convenient it was to blame me, rather than the buffoons that Nasreen Bai had previously chosen.

"I think someone has jinxed the house, they don't want Nadia married," Nasreen Bai emphasized. "But, oh, I am so glad we have it resolved. I have a good feeling about this. Nadia will get to know him better over the next few months and by the time the wedding comes around, they will be much in love."

Nadia seemed happy about her engagement. She wasn't allowed to go out alone with Tariq, but a few chaperoned outings and phone calls were allowed, so every few days she would drag the phone from the end table in the living room to the hallway outside her room for privacy and talk to the young man. An engagement party was set for the twentieth of December, two weeks later.

On the day before Nadia's engagement party, as Lal Khan cleaned the car, he fell to the ground dead, his eyes open to the heavens. In years past, I had witnessed all manner of entrances to and departures from the world, but Lal Khan's death was certainly a most curious one.

Lal Khan hadn't even planned to wash the car, but since the driver was running late, he offered to do it. That morning he had woken to the sound of the azaan and drank his customary cup of chai with three and a half teaspoons of sugar. He then bathed and put on his new white suit, in the event that the demands of the day ahead may not offer him a chance to change into proper attire. He then called his mother in Peshawar, to confirm the money he sent his wife had reached her. Then, just as the sun had started to peer from behind the clouds, he filled the bucket with soapy water, retrieved two washcloths from the laundry line, and made his way to the driveway. As he bent down to clean the wheels, his knees creaked, his throat gave a little croak, and he fell to the ground in a heap of freshly laundered white cotton.

The news traveled to the inner house by way of Nisar, who had witnessed the spectacle as he walked through the front gates and turned onto the driveway, the day's groceries in the arms and a melodious tune on his lips. In a state of panic, he dropped the bags, knelt down beside Lal Khan, and shook him fervently to awaken him. Two kilos of milk exploded onto the driveway, spinach leaves lay bruised among the gravel, and several eggplants, potatoes, and green chilies rolled about as Nisar ran inside screaming, "Haji Sahib, Zainab Baji!! May Allah help us!! We are finished!"

Jameela, startled by such a ruckus, wondered if the gardener had been caught stealing again. She grabbed Nisar by the ear as though he was still a ten-year-old child and gave it a good twist.

"You good for nothing. Stop your screamin' or you'll wake up the devil. And take your shoes off before you come into the house."

"Jameela. The devil awakened already! Lal Khan is dead. Irrevocably dead!" He panted; his eyes full of terror as he squirmed to free himself from Jameela's grip. "Aray, let go of my ear!"

"I'm going to complain to your mother," Jameela said. "You've become a liar. Boys who lie to get out of their chores shouldn't expect to get paid."

But it wasn't a lie, of course. It was a most unfortunate incident, and it took place at a most unfortunate time.

The cause of Lal Khan's death was found to be a heart attack and every member of the household had a theory. Too much ghee in his morning paratha, old age, a fight with his brother over their father's inheritance, the curse of a jinn.

It threw the entire household into disarray. Lal Khan had been a familiar face at our front gate since Zainab and Haji Rahmat had moved here. Every morning began with him perched on his rattan stool by the front gate, drinking his cup of tea, and every day drew to a close with him patrolling the grounds with his tasbih in hand. His loss made us feel the prick of mortality.

Haji Rahmat contacted Lal Khan's family in Peshawar and arranged for tickets, so they could come to Karachi for the funeral.

Junaid was visibly disturbed. "I don't think we should live here anymore," he said quietly as he helped Haji Rahmat make funeral arrangements. "I will never be able to walk down the driveway again without picturing Lal Khan laying there, dead."

Haji Rahmat shook his head sadly. "All we can do is pray for him and his family."

Zainab wept and said that a death before the day of her daughter's engagement was a curse. "What if it was the jinn again," she wondered aloud.

Nadia was out of sorts. She dragged the phone from the living room to the hallway outside her room, sat on the floor, and dialed Mariam's number with trembling fingers, and sobbed into the phone.

"It was awful. A heart attack. In the driveway."

"No, I didn't talk to Tariq as yet," she picked at the polish on her nails, distress crawled across her face. For a few seconds, she sat quiet, hugging her knees into her chest, listening to her friend on the other end of the line. Then she said, slowly: "Mariam, but to think that it happened on the very day. I can't help think, what if this is a sign that maybe I shouldn't marry him?"

I could hear Mariam's voice through the earpiece, hyper and agitated, but couldn't make out what she was saying.

"No, I am not overly superstitious," Nadia said. "Yes, of course, I still like him ... okay, sure come over."

She hung up but remained seated on the ground, her hand resting on the shiny brown receiver. She was still sitting there, ten minutes later, when Mariam arrived.

***

After messages were sent that the engagement party was postponed, and Lal Khan's burial had been tended to, Zainab and Mrs. Ahmed struggled to come up with a new date. They decided to skip an official engagement party and just plan for the wedding instead. It seemed that finding a date that worked for both families was harder than it had been to find a groom. Finally, after considering the groom's out-of-town work commitments, hotel reservations, relatives' schedules, florist and caterer availabilities, and the recommended pause from celebrations during the holy month of Ramadan, Mrs. Ahmed and Zainab set the wedding for June 27, 1981, six months later.

149

23

1981

I often wonder what would have happened if Lal Khan hadn't died the day he did. Nadia's engagement would have gone on as planned. Maybe she wouldn't have gotten sick. Maybe Haji Rahmat wouldn't have died. But then again, maybe this was her fate. Maybe it was my fate too, to forever wonder if I was the one to blame for what happened.

Nadia arrived home from university on a Tuesday afternoon, the 20th of January 1981, to voices conversing in the dining room. "Come in, beta," her mother called out. "Look who's here!"

Nadia dropped her satchel in the foyer, smoothed the creases from her kurta, clipped her hair back neatly, and stepped into the room. Aunty Rabab was bent over the dining table, spooning out food. An elderly man in a wheelchair, with his back toward the room, was seated at the table.

"Hello sweetie! How are you?" Aunty said, and then she released the brake on the wheelchair and turned it around to face Nadia.

For a moment, Nadia's face was blank, and then recognition registered. She brought one hand up to her mouth to contain the gasp.

"Can you even believe it?" Aunty said, smiling.

Nadia stood still in the doorway. Zainab's laughter filled the silence.

"My dear child!" Zainab said. "You look like you've seen a ghost! I was also just as shocked when I saw him at first!"

Nadia formed her words slowly, as though hoping they were false.

"Uncle Jee?" she asked.

"Yes!" Zainab continued. "Can you believe it?"

Nadia stammered. "But how? We thought—"

"So did we," Aunty interrupted. "But by the grace of God, miracle of miracles, he is back safe, even when we thought all was lost."

Uncle Jee was nearly unrecognizable. His blue shirt hung on his bony shoulders. His paunch had disappeared, his cheekbones were sunken, and he had grown a beard. His hair was almost entirely white. He seemed to have lost the use of one leg; he could not get up from the wheelchair, and his trousers hung limply over his left knee.

"Why are you in a wheelchair?" Nadia asked.

Aunty answered. "He was in an explosion in Bangladesh. He injured his legs and lost a lot of his memory. That's why we never heard from him during the war. When he was released from prison, he didn't remember who he was. And then finally, someone recognized him and contacted us, and we were able to get him back."

"He can't remember anything?"

"It comes and goes," Aunty said. "Now it seems that he remembers things from his youth, but not as much from the last fifteen years."

Uncle Jee smiled, his nostrils flaring. "Who is this, remind me again?"

"Aray, it's little Nadia, Haji Rahmat, and Zainab's daughter. Have you forgotten her?" Aunty bent down to face him. Then she continued. "We have started therapy for him. Perhaps we can help him recover his memory. But by the grace of God, at least we have him back."

"Come, eat with us dear," Aunty Rabab said. "You must be starving."

The young woman shook her head no and then sat down mechanically on the chair next to her mother.

There was chatter as the afternoon sunlight streamed in through the glass panes, illuminating things we'd much rather not see. A small tear in the upholstery of the dining chairs, a chip in the Bottecino marble by the door, an inconsistency in the paint color where the pipe had burst, and plaster had been repaired and repainted. The painter had mismatched the white paint, and so that patched area looked more yellow than the rest of the wall. Right there, below the jaundiced patch of paint, sat Uncle Jee. He was in his wheelchair, eating his aloo chaat slowly; a drop of chutney sitting like a blemish on the napkin in his lap.

Nadia sat quiet. She appeared exhausted.

"Beta, will you pour a cup of tea for me, please?" Zainab asked her daughter.

"I'll have some tea as well, please," Uncle Jee said from his wheelchair.

Nadia stayed seated as if lost in her thoughts. Zainab nudged her. "*Beta?*"

At her mother's prompting, Nadia stood up and walked over to the tray where the teapot sat. She removed the tea cosy from the pot and filled two cups with the milky drink. She reached over and placed one teacup on the table in front of Uncle Jee.

The sunken old man peered up at her intently through rheumy eyes. He reached out a trembling hand. "Nadia. Of course, I remember you." He smiled, placing his fingers on her arm. "How could I forget?"

At the touch of his fingers to her flesh, Nadia jerked away, as though singed by fire. She swayed, like she would fall to the floor, and grabbed hold of the chair to steady herself.

Zainab noticed. "What's the matter with you?" she asked. "You don't look well."

"I think I'm just tired." Her knuckles were white on the back of the chair.

"You are rather pale, dear," Aunty said. "Must be dehydration. It was boiling hot today. The construction workers at our home left early. I don't know how you youngsters do it, all day out in the sun at university!"

"Why don't you go get some rest? I'll have Jameela bring some fruit up for you."

Nadia did not answer. I could see the tremble in her fingers deepen as she loosened her hold on the chair.

"It's nice to be back." Uncle Jee's slow voice rumbled out into the air. "And it's nice to see you Nadia."

The girl nodded, eyes squeezed shut, and turned around, a blind ballerina. She bent down, picked up her satchel, and walked out.

Nadia stayed in her room for the remainder of the day. She didn't come down for dinner; she said she was not hungry and had too much schoolwork to finish. Jameela brought food to her room, but the rice turned dry and the daal turned cold, and she didn't eat a thing.

I could not come to terms with the day's revelation. Uncle Jee was alive. Were we supposed to feel sorry for him in his crippled state, riddled with amnesia? *By the grace of God*, Aunty had said. He had returned by the grace of God. Khansama could've returned by the grace of God. Javed could've returned by the grace of God. But no, it had been Uncle Jee who had returned. Uncle Jee who had been saved. How dare he sit there in the living room sipping tea and eating aloo chaat? How dare this terrible man be safe when others were not!

***

Nadia woke the next morning with a start. Her wild eyes and translucent skin made me think a nightmare had crossed the

153

thresholds of sleep and followed her into reality. The woolen blankets across her outstretched legs were twisted and wrung tight. As her pinpoint pupils darted about the room, I remembered the eight-year-old girl who used to wake up often in the same fit of fear.

Nadia made her way to the bathroom, where she pulled open the wooden drawers next to the sink, one by one, searching for something. She tossed items out of the way, the pot of Vaseline, the tin of Nivea cream, the packets of black bobby pins, until she found what she was looking for: a large pair of metal scissors, silver and slightly rusted along one edge. She held her hair up, gathered it into a high ponytail, and began hacking at it. Chunks of dark brown hair fell in waves around her, onto the sink and on the floor. When finally her hair was trimmed close to the nape of her neck in some places and grazed her shoulders in jagged tips in others, she set the scissors on the counter and exhaled.

With her hair cropped thus, she reminded me of the Magnificent Barbie, that she had ravaged so many years ago.

***

Meanwhile, downstairs the morning progressed. Zainab bustled about in the kitchen and Haji Rahmat enjoyed a cup of tea. When Nadia entered the breakfast room, Haji Rahmat glanced up at his daughter with a smile and then balked.

"What happened to your hair?" he asked.

Nadia sat down.

Zainab brought in parathas and eggs, calling back over her shoulder to her son. "Junaid, hurry, you must leave for work."

Then she noticed her daughter. "What happened to your hair?" she gasped, her eyes leaping out of their sockets.

The nineteen-year-old looked down at the sunny side egg on her plate, at the perfect circle of the egg yolk. She took a spoon to it and there was an explosion of saffron lava over the egg white.

"Did you cut your hair?"

"Yes."

Zainab looked impatient, annoyed, and confused. "Why?"

Haji Rahmat took a loud slurp of tea. A teaspoon chimed as it fell onto the floor.

Nadia swirled the runny egg yolk all over the plate shunning her parents' distress. "I like it this way."

Zainab slammed the plates on the table, her green, gleaming eyes still on her daughter's hair. "Have you lost your mind?"

"I just needed a change."

"A change?" Zainab shouted. "Wear a different color of nail polish, for God's sake! Buy a new lipstick. Why destroy your hair?"

Nadia stared intensely at the egg yolk on her plate.

"I'm waiting for an answer, Nadia," Zainab ground out through closed teeth.

"Ammi, I can't deal with this now."

"What do you mean, you can't deal with this? What is there to deal with? You shouldn't have cut off your hair! Then there would be nothing to deal with."

"Zainab, let it be," Haji Rahmat said. "That actress on TV, what is her name ... she has a new short haircut. I do believe it's the fashion these days."

Zainab turned her attention from Nadia to her husband. "The *big deal* is that her wedding is in June! That's in five months. Do you think hair grows overnight? The photos are ruined. God help me."

"I don't want to get married," Nadia said quietly.

"You don't *what*?" Zainab's face burned crimson; her eyes fierce.

"I don't want to get married."

"Nadia, did something happen?" Haji Rahmat said, laying his newspaper and teacup on the table. "Did Tariq say something to you?"

"No."

"Then what's wrong? I thought you liked him, you've been talking on the phone with him, right?"

"I just ... I just don't want to be married yet."

"Did you talk to him about it?"

"No."

Haji Rahmat's eyes filled with concern. But Zainab was furious.

"Why do you play with people's emotions this way? What do you plan to do then?" she asked. "Stay single and alone and ruin your life?"

"Ammi, please."

"What is the matter with you? What have I done to deserve this?"

"This has nothing to do with you," Nadia said and burst into tears.

Haji glared at his wife.

"She's upset. Leave her alone, we can talk later," he said.

Zainab threw her napkin on the table and stood up. "You need to talk to your daughter. And drum some sense into her." Then she yelled into the hallway. "Junaid, if you don't get down here this instant, you can go to work without breakfast!"

Haji Rahmat spoke kindly to his daughter. "There is no need to cry. Just eat your breakfast. We will talk about this later when everyone is calm."

Nadia stood and pushed her chair into the table. "I'm not hungry. And I don't want to talk about it anymore." She slammed the kitchen door behind her and made her way to the car.

After a few moments, Junaid appeared running towards the car with an apple in hand. Nadia was sitting in the backseat of the car, sullen.

"What the hell happened to your hair? Why does it look so bad?" he asked her. "And why is Ammi yelling at Abbu at the breakfast table?"

"Junaid, please shut up." she waved him in and then pulled the car door closed. "I don't know why she yells. Get in the car. Let's go. I'm late because of you."

***

That night Zainab had a nightmare.

She woke suddenly, at four a.m., switched on the bedside lamp, and reached over to shake her husband's arm.

"Wake up," she whispered. "I have something to tell you."

Haji Rahmat was a heavy sleeper and didn't budge, so she shook him again.

"Wake. Up."

Startled, almost automatically, he answered, "What happened? Are the children okay?" His eyes were still closed.

"I think there is a jinn in the storage room. That's why Nadia is acting crazy."

He sat up and rubbed the sleep out of his eyes. "What are you talking about?"

"I had a terrible dream. I heard a woman screaming inside the storage room outside. I went to see what had happened but there was no one there. I looked inside, outside, everywhere. I couldn't see anyone but the screaming, oh God, the screaming, it just wouldn't stop."

Zainab covered her face with her hands, as though doing that would help erase the memory of her dream. Haji Rahmat put his arm around her.

"It wasn't real," he said. "It's okay."

She looked at her husband. "No, but it felt so real. This was different. It didn't feel like other dreams."

"You're sweating," he said. He poured water into a cup from the carafe on his bedside table. "Here, have a sip."

157

Zainab waved the cup away. "Listen to me. What if this is the reason for Nadia's odd behavior?" she said and took a deep breath. "One day she is fine, the next day she chops her hair off and doesn't want to get married. And then I have this nightmare—too much of a coincidence. I am convinced she is behaving this way because of the jinn."

"Zainab—"

"Think about it. Can you think of another explanation?"

"Not right now, not in the middle of the night. There are a thousand other explanations. Maybe they had an argument, maybe she got nervous. Getting married is a big step."

"But that haircut? That is not normal behavior."

He shrugged. "Did you talk to Nadia? Or to Tariq's mother?"

"Not yet."

"Should we call off the wedding?"

"No. No need to make a rash decision."

Haji Rahmat checked the time on the digital radio clock on his bedside and gazed sympathetically toward his wife. Her forehead and hairline were damp with sweat, and she looked physically exhausted.

"Don't worry," he said and gave his wife a kiss. "We will figure it out in the morning. Try to go back to sleep."

"The woman screaming in the shed," she whispered, after a few minutes of silence. "It sounded like Nadia."

Haji Rahmat inhaled sharply and faced his wife. "No. It wasn't her. It was a bad dream."

They sat quietly for a few minutes. Haji Rahmat drifted back to sleep but Zainab lay awake in bed. She sat up, propped a pillow behind her back, and reached for a magazine from the stack on her nightstand. Absentmindedly, she flipped through the glossy pages of *The Herald* as she waited for the sun to rise.

Zainab's instinct was correct: she alone realized that what was wrong with Nadia went deeper than a bad mood, a haircut on a whim, and a sudden urge to break off her engagement. And yet, Zainab was at a loss when it came to the why of Nadia's behavior. And having no reason, she had taken her dream as an omen, that meddling by the supernatural was the default explanation for her daughter's behavior. I wished she had asked Nadia more questions, wondered about it more, gone over the events of the past days a little more carefully. Because in her analysis, what Zainab had missed was the idea that perhaps the jinn were warning us, rather than harming us.

That morning after her husband left for work, Zainab supervised a thorough cleaning of the storage room. It housed the leftovers; extra chairs stacked atop dusty side tables, old wicker furniture that was waiting to be mended and reused, boxes of old newspapers, extra tile, and scraps of wood from the library renovation. Anything that didn't have a place had over the years found its way into the storage room. Jameela and Nisar cleaned it out and removed all the leftover odds and ends. The newspapers and old magazines were sold by the kilo to be recycled or burned, and Nisar loaded the furniture into the rental Suzuki truck that would deliver it to those who could put it to good use.

The room was now empty, heavy only with the weight of that which we could not see. Jameela recommended lighting incense to purify the space. If there was a jinn in the room, she said, perhaps we could appease it. The small rectangular window by the ceiling was cranked open and Jameela lit half a box of Metromilan Agarbatti. The tips of the incense sticks glowed, wisps of smoke curled up, and the scent of frankincense and screwpine filled the room and drifted out of the open door. Thirty minutes later the incense sticks had been consumed, leaving in their wake the heady, sweet-smelling ash. Zainab shut the door and locked it from the outside with an iron padlock.

***

That same day, at about half-past twelve, the university headmaster phoned to inform that Nadia had fainted.

159

Zainab called Haji Rahmat at the factory, and then rushed to the college. They returned at four p.m., Haji Rahmat and Zainab with their daughter held between them.

"What is wrong with her?" Jameela asked, frantic.

"We don't know," Zainab said, after settling her daughter in her room. "We took her to the hospital, and they believe it was perhaps dehydration. The nurse will come to administer an IV later tonight."

Junaid arrived that evening with the home care nurse. Tests had been inconclusive, but Nadia was now running a fever; the doctor prescribed Paracetamol and antibiotics for the stomachache that had come on as well. She barely ate or drank, so the nurse agreed to return the following day to check her vitals and administer another IV as needed.

Zainab stayed with her that night, layering cool, damp towels that smelled of eau de cologne on Nadia's forehead to bring her fever down. She stroked her daughter's short, abrasive haircut.

"I didn't mean to yell at you about your hair," she said softly. "It's just I have so much on my mind these days, with all the wedding preparations. It threw me off."

A few minutes later she continued. "I know you don't want to get married. But will you think about it? Don't make rash decisions just yet."

Nadia's eyes were closed, and I don't know if she heard her mother. I wondered what she thought about as she slept, and what fears crippled her. Tariq had heard that she had fainted at school, and had called several times that day, and Zainab had told him Nadia was resting but doing alright. The fortunate thing was that contact between them was limited to a few phone calls, and societal propriety still dictated that the betrothed not meet in person before the wedding, so we could get away with being discreet and offering little information.

Zainab closed her eyes and fell asleep on the chair at Nadia's bedside. Suddenly, she woke up, startled at the movement. Nadia had sat up violently in bed, and the force of her hand had knocked over the pitcher of water on the nightstand.

"What's the matter?" Zainab said. "What happened?"

Nadia searched the room with her eyes, gasping. "I ... I just had a bad dream. Who just came in the room?"

"No one."

Nadia looked around unconvinced and then pulled the blanket over her head.

Zainab appeared worried. "Here, it's time for your medicine," she said, and carefully folded back the blanket and handed Nadia the pink tablet, then picked up the glass and wiped the water that had fallen on the floor.

Nadia took the medicine, swallowed it slowly, and wrapped the woolen blanket tightly around herself.

Zainab spent the next few nights in Nadia's room. Every few hours, Nadia sat up with a start, rigid and tense, staring straight ahead as though someone had a gun to her head. A few minutes later, she relaxed, as though the terror had passed. She'd lie back down, shivering under blankets that Zainab tucked around her. "What happens to you?" Zainab would ask. Nadia would not answer. As she floated back to sleep, Zainab prayed Surah Yaseen over her daughter.

Haji Rahmat worried incessantly. He had no way to console his daughter.

"I don't know what to believe," Zainab said, "but the way she behaves at night is really like someone possessed."

Haji Rahmat disagreed. "I think she's just worried about something."

"Nasreen Bai thinks someone has put evil eye, nazr, on her," Zainab continued. "The Ahmeds are such a good family, everyone wants their daughter to marry their son."

Haji Rahmat sighed.

"I'm going to call Apa this evening," Zainab said after a moment's pause. "She can bring some herbal remedies and pray on her," Zainab said.

"Yes, let's try that," he replied. "I'm also going to consult with another doctor."

Haji Rahmat spent evenings at his daughter's bedside. He read to her and tried to force her to join him in the garden for his evening walk. She would last ten minutes before returning to her room. A week later, the fever broke, and we were hopeful. But we traded fever for melancholy.

Since Nadia had not been going to school, and exams were approaching, Mariam came over with her schoolbooks to help her study.

"Did Tariq say something to you?" Mariam asked as she tried peer past the doorway into Nadia's dimly lit room. "Be honest with me, because if he did, I will have my brother beat him up so bad he won't know what hit him."

Nadia shook her head no and offered a small smile at her friend's attempt to cheer her up. We all knew that Mariam's brother was a timid ten-year-old.

Nadia gratefully took the books, but didn't spend any time with her friend, saying that she needed to sleep.

Many days went by this way, with Nadia keeping to herself in her room, lingering between sleep and semi-consciousness.

The doctor came for a house call.

"Is it jaundice?" Haji Rahmat asked.

"No, I don't think so. Is she worried about something?" the doctor speculated. "Is there something happening at school? Are studies too much for her?"

"She's always excelled academically," Haji Rahmat said. "I can't imagine it could be that."

"The broken sleep, the nightmares, it may be related to some trauma or fear she has. I would say she is suffering from depression." The doctor continued, "I can prescribe some medicine."

It bothered Zainab to hear the word *depression* used for her daughter. "Depression?" she said. "Why would my daughter have that? Your diagnosis makes no sense. She is beautiful, well-liked by everyone, has enough friends, and does well at school. She cannot have *depression.*"

"Mrs. Rahmat, I don't know what else to tell you. See if you can talk to her, to figure out what is bothering her. The medication will help calm her anxiety and help her sleep better."

"It's not depression," Zainab later said to her husband. "I'll believe sooner that a jinn has taken over her than she's suffering from depression. These doctors love to over-analyze and over-medicate."

Haji Rahmat said nothing, but the worry was apparent in his eyes.

Later, on their evening walk around the garden, Haji Rahmat asked Nadia what was worrying her.

Nadia appeared as if she wanted to speak but had no words.

"You can tell me anything," he prompted.

"I know I can, Abbu," she said. She stopped in her tracks and looked up at her father. Haji Rahmat enveloped his daughter in a hug and held her close.

"Can I go back to my room now?"

Haji Rahmat's face sagged in disappointment. "Being in your room all the time is making you worse," he said.

I suffered under the burden of knowledge. How did no one else see what was so obvious to me?

"Your friends are missing you. They call all the time. Yesterday they came to see you, but you were sleeping. Tariq has called, too, many times."

Nadia didn't respond. She seemed to be lost in her thoughts.

"Have you told him you want to end the engagement?"

"No. Not yet."

Haji Rahmat sighed in relief. "Your exams start next week. I don't know if you're ready, so I will ask Mrs. Joseph if you can take them later, or perhaps at home?"

At that, Nadia suddenly snapped back into reality.

"My exams? What day is it?" she asked.

"The 3rd of May. You've been taking a lot of medicine. It's not surprising you lost track of time."

"I'll go for my exams," Nadia said. "I'm ready."

The worry lines on Haji Rahmat's forehead relaxed. She hadn't called off her engagement, and she was ready to go back to college to take her exams; surely, these were good signs. As a drowning man clutches at a straw, it was clear that he saw these as rays of hope. I must confess that I did, too.

***

A few days later, Tariq and his sister surprised us with a visit.

"Sorry to stop by unannounced," he said shifting uncomfortably in the doorway. "We were in the neighborhood and wanted to drop these off for you." His sister who stood next to him presented Zainab with a silver tray filled with an assortment of pastries and savories.

"Oh, these look delicious, thank you!" Zainab said. "Won't you come in?"

Tariq's happy smile revealed that he was counting on her hospitality. "Is Nadia home?" he asked shyly. "I thought I might say hello and see how she is doing? We haven't talked for a while." He held a bouquet of pink roses in his hand.

Zainab smiled but her eyes betrayed the worry that she felt, probably at the prospect of coaxing her daughter out of her room. She had the guests sit in the drawing room, and, with her husband, went to get Nadia.

"You don't have to see them if you don't want to, but he's come all this way," Haji Rahmat said gently to his daughter. "Maybe just see him for a few minutes?"

To all of our surprise, Nadia was ready.

"I'll see them," she said quickly. "I just need to change."

Haji Rahmat's eyes widened in surprise. I know he had probably thought of several other things to convince her to come out. I couldn't allow myself to feel happy and wondered if she was planning to tell Tariq that the engagement was off. It was so hard to know with her those days.

In her bathroom, Nadia washed up, put on a sky-blue kurta and some white pants, took care with her hair, and put on a pair of pearl earrings before she went to greet the guests.

"You cut your hair," Tariq said, kindly, when she came into the living room. "Very post-modern." He handed her the flowers with a shy smile. "These are for you."

"Thank you." Nadia smiled in appreciation at the roses. She combed her fingers through her hair, a little awkwardly. "The hair, yes." She tried to laugh. "I figured; less is more."

Tariq laughed. His eyes shone to see her, and I could tell he was completely taken in by Nadia. The three of them sat together in the living room, Tariq's sister an unwanted chaperone.

"Are you feeling alright?" he asked Nadia.

"Yes. Just a lot of headaches. I'll be okay."

"You've lost weight, Nadia," his sister observed. "Is it in preparation for the wedding?"

"Uh, yes, sure," Nadia mumbled.

Tariq gave his sister a disapproving look.

The sister laughed to fill the uncomfortable silence and handed Nadia a white pastry box decorated with a festive silver bow. "We brought some chocolate biscuits," she said. "Tariq says they are your favorite."

Nadia smiled at her fiancé. "You remembered," she said to him. "How sweet."

I waited anxiously to see if Nadia would bring up the engagement, but she did not. I allowed myself to believe that was a good sign.

***

The next morning, the day of her exams, Nadia woke up early. She showered and put on her gray uniform and gathered her books. She pinned her dupatta onto her kurta and headed for breakfast.

Zainab and Haji Rahmat could barely conceal their joy to see her outside her room without any pleading and coaxing. It was as though a weight had been lifted off their shoulder. One would think they had just welcomed a child returned home from months away at war.

"Good morning. What a pleasure to see you!" Haji Rahmat said. "What would you like for breakfast?"

"I'm not actually that hungry," Nadia said as she gave her father a kiss goodbye.

"You mustn't go to school on an empty stomach! Here, eat some almonds for energy." And he pressed a fistful of almonds into her palm.

"Let me drop you off at school, Nadia," Zainab said.

"Ammi, please, I'm twenty. I don't need you to drop me off."

Zainab smiled. For a second, Nadia sounded like her old self. She gave her daughter a hug. "Okay fine. Good luck."

Zainab thought to take advantage of the situation and supervised a quick clean-up of her daughter's bedroom. It was often hard to get Nadia out, and sometimes her room didn't get cleaned for days. Zainab surveyed her daughter's space; the closets were messy with upturned clothes, and piles and piles of books lay scattered over her desk and on the bed. She began to gather the books. A book of Rubaiyat lay under the pillow, open on the page where Nadia had underlined the following verse:

بُجھتی ہی نہیں شمع ، جلے جاتی ہے

کٹتی ہی نہیں رات ، ڈھلے جاتی ہے

جاری ہے نفس کی آ مدوشد فانی

سینے میں چُھری ہے کہ چلے جاتی ہے

فَانی بدایونی

The taper doth not expire, but burns and burns,
The night doth not come to end, on its wheel it turns,
While the breath goes in and out, I seem to feel,
That a dagger in my breast to and fro doth run.
-Fani Badayuni

Worry flickered across Zainab's eyes as she snapped the book shut and placed it atop the stack of books on her daughter's desk. She gathered the empty teacups from the bedside table and noticed several empty blister packs in the drawer. Nadia had been sending for sleeping aids on her own. Zainab also noticed tally marks above the bedside, marked with pen on the wall.

Nisar changed the bed linens, aired out the blankets, and fluffed the pillows in the room. When the room had been cleaned, Zainab had a stern conversation with the staff—no one was to go to the pharmacy on Nadia's behalf without informing Zainab first.

An hour later, Nadia returned home from her exams and headed straight to her room.

"You're back early," Haji Rahmat said as he saw her walk by. "How were the exams?"

"Not good." Nadia disappeared behind her room door. Then there was the click of the key turning in the lock.

Haji Rahmat contemplated for a few minutes. Then he went outside.

"Why has Nadia returned so soon?" he asked the driver.

The driver looked troubled. "We drove to school, but she wouldn't get out of the car. So, then we sat there, outside the school gate for half an hour and I waited for Baji to get out. I asked her if she was okay. At first, she didn't answer, but then, she insisted I bring her back home."

Nadia didn't return to university after that day.

Zainab requested a medical leave, and we waited for Nadia to get better. Some days she seemed like her old self, going outside, and eating meals with the family, catching up on schoolwork, walking in the garden. But there were other days which she spent all alone in the deafening silence of her bedroom, sleeping, ignoring the knocks on her door, and shunning any interaction. Sometimes she woke from sleep with a start, mumbling things to herself, looking wildly around the room. Some days, she would pace her room in anxiety, or stay in her bed scribbling in her notebook, making tally marks on the wall.

When Mariam came by with some friends from school, Nadia would not open her bedroom door.

"I think she must be asleep," Zainab said awkwardly as they stood outside her bedroom door. "You are so sweet to come visit her."

"She won't return my phone calls," Mariam said. "You told her I called, right?"

"Yes, of course, I'm sure she meant to call you back, she just must have forgotten."

It appeared from Mariam's expression that she did not believe Zainab.

"I'll let her know you came by when she wakes up."

"I hope she feels better." Mariam sighed and knocked once more.

Inside, Nadia crouched on the floor in her bedroom, her back against the door, her palms pressed against her ears as though to block out their voices.

***

Through it all, Nadia had still not canceled the wedding.

168

June brought longer days and shorter nights. The wedding date drew closer, and the Ahmeds wanted to bring gifts. Zainab had tried a number of times to postpone the gift-giving because she knew Nadia was not up to meeting so many people, but Mrs. Ahmed was ramping up from impatient to annoyed and so Zainab gave in. They would arrive, Mrs. Ahmed and some of the women of her family, on the evening of the fourth.

"It'll just be an hour, I promise," Zainab said to Nadia. "You don't have to talk much, no one expects the bride-to-be to do much talking. It's a formality. Just come sit with them for a few minutes and then you can leave."

Nadia did not show any enthusiasm.

"Here, you can wear this. Tariq's family sent it for you." She held up a delicately embroidered blouse and an aquamarine sari edged with pearls. "I'll have Jameela iron it for you."

Nadia stared dully at the bridal outfit.

"You'll be okay, my dear," Zainab said. "Be strong."

That evening, facing her future family, Nadia's face was drawn with exhaustion. She sat with her trembling hands tucked into the crevices of the sofa cushions and managed only to smile and nod when someone spoke to her. Before the party, Haji Rahmat had sat with her and given her a pep talk, Jameela had done strings of prayers on her, and Zainab had reminded Nadia to take her anxiety medication. But even with the joint effort of the whole household behind her, Nadia was far from her usual self. This did not go unnoticed.

Everyone smiled and laughed and gushed over the gifts: an emerald choker, a set of gold bangles encrusted with rubies, two diamond and pearl earrings, and three exquisite saris sat amongst mounds of elegantly decorated sweetmeats. The guests nibbled on mushroom and cheese vol au vents, chocolate eclairs, and apple tarts, but on their way out to their cars, they whispered about Nadia: *What was wrong? Was she unwell? Was she unhappy with the arrangement? Had the boy and girl had an argument?*

***

169

The gift-presenting event had decimated what little composure Nadia had mustered. The breaking point had been reached. Even Zainab felt that they had no choice—the wedding could not take place next week. She invited Tariq's mother for coffee the next day.

Mrs. Ahmed knew the reason for the meeting. "My son told me when he last talked to Nadia, she said she wanted to postpone the wedding." Mrs. Ahmed fiddled with the enormous ruby ring on her finger. "What's going on?"

"Our daughter has not been keeping that well."

"And so she wants to postpone the wedding?"

"Oh, yes, they may have discussed postponement," Zainab said.

"It wasn't a discussion, per se. The idea was one-sided, initiated by your daughter."

Zainab sniffed and stared at the rug, uncomfortable. "The truth of the matter is she has been rather unwell for the past few weeks, and even the party yesterday was exhausting for her. So, keeping that in mind, we'd like to propose a short delay."

Deep wrinkles spread across Mrs. Ahmed's forehead. She pursed her lips. "I see."

"We just think it would be better for her to be well enough for her own event, think about what people would say if she showed up looking pale and miserable?"

"My dear Zainab, people are already talking. They have begun to say that there is something wrong with our boy and that is why the girl's side keeps postponing."

Haji Rahmat interjected. "Rashida, we both know that's not true. It shouldn't matter what people are saying."

"What's the diagnosis?" Mrs. Ahmed asked.

"Diagnosis?"

"You said she isn't well. What's the diagnosis?"

While Zainab seemed to be considering her words, Haji Rahmat answered quickly. "There is none. The doctor says she just is dealing with some anxiety."

"But it's under control," Zainab added, glaring at him. She didn't like the word *anxiety* to be used when describing Nadia. Zainab felt that *anxiety*, and that word the doctor had used before, *depression,* were nothing more than euphemisms for madness.

"My brother is a doctor," Mrs. Ahmed offered. "He can help."

"No, it's not that—she just needs a little time," Zainab said.

"You know, Zainab," Mrs. Ahmed said, "this sounds like you're making excuses. Are you not interested in our son?"

"That is not the case. We are very fond of your son, and so is Nadia."

"Then what is the problem?"

"I just told you. She is not well. We think she simply needs a few weeks, and then she'll be back on her feet."

"Our guests have already booked their tickets. Some are in town; many others are on their way. Zainab, are we to send them away again?"

Zainab was silent.

"You know, it seems to me you are looking for a reason to call it off," she said hotly. "First your driver dies and you call off the engagement abruptly. Now Nadia is 'sick', but you won't tell us what is wrong. And she has been ignoring my son's phone calls. Well, we hear you loud and clear. We are not good enough for you. We will call it off. There are plenty of young girls who would be delighted and honored to marry our son."

Mrs. Ahmed pursed her lips grimly as she spoke, like one used to getting her way. She was puffed with decades of pride and her face had a smirk as though she had twisted the nail that needed twisting, and now Nadia's parents would buckle.

Zainab was taken aback. "That is not at all what we are saying."

"It sounds to me like that is exactly what you are saying."

"Please be reasonable, Rashida. This is our children's future! Don't be so rash. Let's move it to winter of this year. That's just six months. She will be well by then."

"Zainab, has your daughter lost her mind? Because that's what I'm hearing. And I don't like to hear from outsiders that my son's bride-to-be is mentally unstable."

"No, God forbid," Zainab said, horrified. "Who said that?"

"You need to be honest with me. Either we go on as planned, or if the rumor that she really is mentally unstable is true, then the is wedding off," Mrs. Ahmed said.

Haji Rahmat stared at his guest with disdain. "Mrs. Ahmed," he said, standing up. "If this is all it takes for you to call it off, then so be it. We are not indebted to you, and we certainly are not asking for any favors."

Zainab whispered harshly to her husband under her breath and put her hand on his arm, to hold him back.

"Please," she said. "Let's all be reasonable here."

"*We* are being reasonable," Haji Rahmat said to his wife. "And honest. My daughter is sick. We're respectfully asking for some time. Mrs. Ahmed is the one being difficult. She has made clear the kind of person she is, and more than that, she has made it clear that she does not care about our daughter's well-being."

"I will not sit here and be disrespected by you, Haji Rahmat." Mrs. Ahmed stood to face him squarely. "I won't accept it. I am leaving and will let my son and husband know of this." She gathered her sari and picked up her purse. With a dramatic air, she exited the room, making sure to slam the door.

Zainab was mortified. "What have you done? Nadia agrees to one boy out of seven, and you ruin her chance of finally getting married!"

Haji Rahmat harrumphed and then casually perused the tea trolley. "Zainab. Get a hold of yourself. That family may be rich, but they have no class. What rubbish behavior. I don't want my daughter to be married into that household. Frankly, it's their loss. Now, tell me, what sort of sandwiches are these?"

"What is the matter with you? Go and stop Mrs. Ahmed and tell her you are sorry. And set a date for the wedding. We cannot let her leave like this!"

"I will do no such thing, Zainab. Mrs. Ahmed is devoid of decency. I want nothing to do with that woman or her son. Nadia deserves better."

Zainab ran from the drawing room, toward the front gate. "Rashida!" she called. "Wait a minute. We can figure this out."

Mrs. Ahmed did not hesitate as she slid into her waiting car, gave Zainab a cold stare, then shut the door and motioned to the chauffeur to drive away.

24

Haji Rahmat died on the 14th of December 1981, from a heart attack. It had been 11 months since Uncle Jee returned, 11 months since Nadia had taken ill, and 6 months since her wedding had been called off. If things had gone according to plan, perhaps we would have heard the news that Nadia was expecting, and that Haji Rahmat and Zainab would soon be grandparents. But here we were, mourning a death.

The jasmine hedges that lined the exterior shed their flowers to form a fragrant white carpet outside Haji Rahmat's bedroom window. The garden crows, generally given to rude, cacophonous dissent, were silent. The trees held their breath. That night even the crickets paid their respects, giving us respite from their incessant chirping.

We made arrangements for the funeral. A large tent, the sort used for weddings, was pegged in the front to provide shade for the mourners. But large as it was, it contained neither our grief, nor the onslaught of grievers. They dotted the foyer, and the drawing and dining rooms. They huddled together on the rugs, prayer beads sifting through their fingers. They punctuated the sofas and chairs, as they sat reading the Quran. They whispered to each other and dabbed their eyes. They spilled out through the front door onto the marble veranda, and through the iron gates onto the street. Despair snaked through fingers pressed tightly together in prayer. Melancholy and curiosity tiptoed between hushed voices: *it was not time,* they said, and *what will the family do,* and *he must have died of sorrow to see his daughter this way,* and *at least he left a sizable fortune behind,* and *all this money, but they can't cure the daughter,* and *has she gone mad?*

As prayers were said and prayer beads counted, as some paid their respects and as others cried, as Haji Rahmat lay in his bed for one last time wrapped in his burial cloth, peaceful and luminescent, a smile on his face, I wondered what my fate would be. And when his coffin was carried out of the room on the shoulders of his loved ones, and he left the home he loved so much, the finality of it hit me with a leaden blow, and I, too, wept as though I had lost a father.

25

Nisar is sitting idle in the kitchen because there isn't much to do. It has been three months since Haji Rahmat's funeral. Junaid is at work, and Nadia ... well, Nadia is in her room, as usual, so rather than eat alone on the dining table, Zainab asks for her lunch to be brought to her room. Jameela takes the tray upstairs. The smell of the curry and potatoes is strong and lingers around the wrought iron banisters of the staircase for several minutes after Jameela passed through. In Zainab's bedroom, Jameela sets the tray of food on the wooden table next to the armchair and turns to leave, but Zainab, who has just finished her prayers, motions for her to stay.

"Have you seen her today?" she asks, hopeful.

"No," Jameela answers. "I left her breakfast outside her room, but she hasn't opened her door all morning."

Zainab puts a limp hand to her forehead, distraught. "What am I going to do?" she says. "Jameela, tell me. Be honest. What do you think? Is she getting better or worse?"

Jameela pauses for a moment before answering. "Some days she seems better."

Zainab gets up from the prayer mat. The curtains are all drawn except one, and the room is dark.

"He just died and left me–with all this."

"Baji, come now, eat some food."

Zainab sits down on the armchair. She removes the lid off the small silver vessel on the tray and spoons some curry, yellow and creamy, on her plate. She tears a two-inch piece of naan, dips it in the curry, and takes a bite. "Not enough salt," she says and sets the plate to the side.

Jameela has settled cross-legged on the rug a few feet from the armchair.

She shakes her head in disapproval. "Baji," she says, "there is much to be done, if you don't eat, you will have no energy."

"I think I'll lie down and take a nap."

But she has only just rested her head on her pillow when Nisar comes upstairs with the message that Uncle Jee and Aunty have come to visit.

"Oh," she sighs. "Have them sit in the drawing room. And make some tea. I'll be down in a few minutes."

Zainab goes to the bathroom and turns on the tap, letting the water run for a few minutes. She watches it trickle down the basin. When it is warm, she wets a washcloth, wrings it out, and presses it against her face. She bends over the sink, leaning on her elbows, face in the washcloth for a few minutes. Then, as though it is the hardest thing to do, she lifts her head, pats her face dry, and proceeds to change her clothes. She checks her reflection in the mirror, smooths her hair, and covers it with the dupatta. Before she leaves her room, she reaches for the blister pack of Paracetamol on her nightstand, presses out two tablets in the palm of her hand, and swallows them with a sip of water.

Nadia waits in her bedroom by the door, listening. She is waiting till she is sure it is quiet, until Jameela has finished her chores, and Zainab has gone in her room for her mid-afternoon nap. She'd rather not see anyone or be drawn into conversation. It is only when she finds the house quiet, that she comes out of her room to go into the kitchen to make herself some tea. Or she strolls in the garden, picking at flowers. At the slightest sound—of the kitchen door opening or Jameela shouting at Nisar, she leaps in fear and darts like an injured gazelle to her room, back into hiding.

Nadia hasn't heard Nisar's announcement to her mother, so she probably assumes her mother will be napping. After standing at her bedroom door for several minutes, she opens it carefully. As it creaks, ever so slightly, and I wonder when someone, anyone would remember to oil the hinges.

Out in the hallway to the kitchen, Nadia runs into her mother, who is on her way to meet the guests.

"Beta," Zainab begins. "Jameela said you didn't eat this morning. Are you hungry? She made your favorite curry for lunch."

"Oh," Nadia says, confused. "I ... I just woke up. What time is it?"

Zainab bites her lip. I know she wants to tell Nadia that sleeping all day is unhealthy, that she needs to have a better schedule, and that she has to make an effort to get better. I know this because she has told her daughter this many times before, and although it has never helped, I know Zainab wants to say it again anyway because, really, what else is there to say? But the doctor has told her to choose her battles. *Don't pick on everything your daughter does,* he has told her. *Give her some time. She will get better.* So Zainab says nothing.

It is as though Nadia knows what is on her mother's mind, and embarrassed she replies to unspoken words. "The medicine," she says. "It makes me drowsy."

Zainab sighs. She has argued with the doctor about the medication he prescribes. *I don't want my daughter on addictive medication,* she has told him. *She is so young.* But he has said it is essential to calm her.

"Aunty and Uncle Jee are here," Zainab says brightly, to change the subject. "Come greet them. Last week when they came to visit, Uncle Jee was asking about you."

Nadia takes a deep, shuddering breath and closes her eyes. Her jaw clenches. Unclenches. Clenches. "I don't want to see them."

"Don't be rude. What will they think? Go on, change your clothes, and come."

Nadia says nothing; her body appears to contract, to shrink into the floor.

"You're going to have to start interacting with people, Nadia," Zainab presses on. You're going to have to start acting... normal. How long will this go on? You're always in your room. Always on the verge of being upset. I don't know how to help you! And now with Abbu gone, I can't do this on my own."

Nadia's face shutters. Her mother cannot see the anguish I know is battering her insides. Zainab continues.

"Uncle Jee is always asking about you. And I always have to make excuses. After all he has done for us, Nadia! I must insist, today you must come, give them a greeting and check in on his health. Is that too much to ask?"

From her face, I can see we have lost her. She has slipped away. Nadia turns away from her mother, floats back to her room. "I don't want to see him." Her voice is a breath, only I can hear.

***

Nadia locks her door. The curtains are drawn, and the room is dark as usual except for the unsettling glow that emanates from the lava lamp on the nightstand. She goes into the bathroom, turns on the faucet, and pushes the drain stop into the base of the cast iron bathtub. Her palms have white crescent imprints in them from clenching her hands so tight, and the skin around her fingernails is raw and blistered. The faucet gurgles and sputters; then a steady stream of water issues forth and the tub begins to fill. Nadia sits at the edge of the tub, waiting. Her feet are pale against the pink floor tiles. The fluorescent bathroom light draws unwanted attention to her hollow cheekbones and dulled skin. Three days ago, on Jameela's insistence, Nadia reluctantly agreed to let her oil her hair, but since then it has become matted.

The water level in the tub begins to rise. Eventually, it reaches the molded rim and starts to spill over, soaking the shaggy, rose-colored bathmat. Nadia pivots her legs into the bathtub. She leans her back against the tiled wall, and closes her eyes, as though contemplating her next move. Tears flow forcefully through her closed eyelids. She grips the sides of the bathtub and slowly begins to lower herself in. The water seeps through her cotton pants, and the hem of her kurta, darkening the floral pattern on her clothes.

Suddenly, the bathroom window swings open with force and bangs against the wall. The glass in the pane cracks down the middle. Startled by the sound, Nadia's eyes flutter open. She clasps the rim of the bathtub tighter and pulls herself up. She looks around and catches sight of herself in the brass mirror that hangs over the pedestal sink. From her perch at the molded rim, half-submerged in the tub, she stares at her reflection for a long time. Then, unresolved turmoil gives way to a flash of determination; her jaw tenses, and her tired eyes brighten momentarily with resolve.

Nadia hoists herself out of the bathtub, and dashes out of the room with urgency. The water is still running, and her clothes are dripping and clinging to her gaunt body but that does not seem to concern her. She runs down the stairs towards the front of the house, leaving wet footprints on the floors and the carpets in her wake. The sound of voices engaged in muted conversation float in from the drawing room; Aunty, Uncle Jee, and Zainab are talking about the finances at the yarn factory. Nadia does not go toward the voices. Instead, she runs through the kitchen, out the side door, past the washbasins. She doesn't stop running until she gets to the storage room.

The sky bows under the heavyweight of the clouds, ripping at the edges. A few drops of rain fall from the sky and awaken the earth.

The door to the storage room is bolted. A thick metal chain is wrapped twice around the lock and secured with a padlock. A large shovel leans against the door.

Nadia picks up the shovel and swings it with full force at the lock. She misses, and the shovel hits the door, making a groove in the wood. She swings repeatedly, hitting the doorknob, the lock, and the chain with an ancient anger. A neighbor looking over the wall would believe her unhinged, and yet I know that is not the case, because today, after years, I see a fierce clarity and determination in her eyes.

26

In the drawing room, Aunty Rabab consoles Zainab, and Uncle Jee, huddled in his wheelchair, talks about things he can recall. He remembers the sound of Haji Rahmat's laugh, his astute business acumen. Zainab smiles at the fond memories of her husband.

The front gate swings open and a car drives in, windshield wipers slowly swishing at the smattering of raindrops. Junaid has just come home from work.

"What's that noise coming from the back?" he asks Nisar, who doesn't know, so Junaid jogs to the back of the house. The rain is getting stronger. He sees his sister, banging the shovel into the door.

"Nadia," he calls out. "What are you doing?"

She doesn't hear him, or perhaps she chooses not to answer. Wood splinters fly around her.

"Go call Ammi," he yells to Nisar and breaks into a run. The clouds drop thick raindrops on him, on the shed, on his sister.

"What is the matter with you?" he cries, when he gets to her. She hacks away at the door, as if to eliminate an enemy. He tries to take the shovel from his sister's hand and is surprised at the strength with which she is gripping it. He tries to hold her arms back, but as she swings the shovel with force he ducks out of the way.

The wooden door splits down the middle and swings open.

Nadia drops the shovel on the ground and stares into the shed.

"Nadia." He steps in front of his sister. "Look at me. What's wrong?"

"It's empty," she says.

"Yes, it is. Ammi emptied it out a year ago, remember? What are you looking for?" He puts his arm around her. "Nadia, come with me, let's go inside please."

Nisar and Zainab come running, followed by Aunty Rabab pushing Uncle Jee in his wheelchair. The old man bumps up and down in the seat.

Zainab stops and puts her hands to her head. "What is this?"

Nadia scans the group of people who have gathered. She looks at her mother, then Aunty, and then Uncle Jee, sitting in the wheelchair.

"You," she says slowly, pointing to Uncle Jee with the shovel. "You should've died in the war. In Bangladesh. Why did you come back?"

"Nadia!" Zainab gasps. "How can you say something like this?"

Everyone is quiet. The raindrops splashing on the leaves of the trees seem inordinately loud.

"Junaid, please take Nadia inside, I'll be right there," Zainab says, and then turns to Uncle Jee and Aunty. "I'm so sorry, Nadia is not herself today. Please, let's all go back inside."

Nadia squirms to break free of Junaid's grasp. "Ask him," she says. She throws down the shovel. Her voice rises to a shriek. "Ask Uncle Jee. Ask him what he did when I was seven, and we were playing hide-and-seek. Tell them, Uncle Jee. Tell them what you did when you took me to hide in this room."

Zainab turns back to face her daughter. Her mouth hangs open in confusion, but horror has begun creeping into her eyes. Junaid puts his hands on Nadia's shoulders, giving her just a little shake, his eyes boring into hers.

"Nadia, what are you talking about?" he whispers.

"What is the matter with her?" Aunty says. "What is she saying?"

Heads swivel, all eyes on Uncle Jee now, everyone expecting a response. "Nadia, beta," he rasps. "Is everything alright? I don't know what you are talking about."

The rain has turned the dry sand on the ground into mulch. The clouds are dark.

"That's just perfect, isn't it?" Nadia steps away from Junaid. She is trembling. "You come back from the dead and have forgotten everything. I had just begun to convince myself that it wasn't me, that it wasn't my fault. And then you show up. And it begins all over again. The paranoia. The guilt. The shame." She jabs a pale finger at him. "I wish you were dead."

Aunty claps her hand over her mouth in shock. "Beta!" she says. "Take hold of yourself. I think you've confused Uncle Jee with someone else." She turns to Zainab. "Maybe it is a jinn ... the poor girl."

Zainab looks at Uncle Jee, then Aunty. And she looks at her daughter. A slew of emotions flicker across her face—confusion, horror, anger, betrayal.

"Ammi—" Nadia drops to the ground now and is sitting in a heap, pleading with her mother for comfort, like a small child. Junaid sits with her, holding her tight, trying to stop the tremors that convulse through his sister's body. He locks eyes with Uncle Jee.

"Is that true?" he asks.

"You can't possibly believe her," Aunty Rabab says. "She's going through a mental breakdown. Poor child needs help. Shall I call for an ambulance?"

Nadia looks only at her mother. The rain stops as suddenly as it began. A few sparrows circle in the sky overhead, calling out.

"There is no need for an ambulance," Zainab says slowly. "You both need to leave my house right now." She turns to her daughter. "I believe you."

Aunty stammers. "Zainab. Have you lost your mind, too? I understand it is traumatic to have one's child say something like this, but please."

Zainab glowers at Uncle Jee. "I don't understand any of this. When and how. Or most of all why. I have respected you my whole life, but—" Zainab stops herself short. She closes her eyes and buries her face in her hands.

"Zainab!" Aunty says. "How can you disrespect us like this? Have some compassion. He is suffering."

Zainab lifts her head, squares her shoulders, and spits out, "We are all way beyond compassion now. And do not talk to me about suffering." Then she bends over Uncle Jee. "Have you really lost your memory?" she asks the old man, slowly forming the words as though there is a disconnect between her mind and her mouth. "Or is this a facade? Like the one you have been putting on with us over the years. Pretending to be part of our family, all the while—"

Uncle Jee cuts her off. "I don't know what you are accusing me of. Nadia is like my daughter."

Junaid lunges towards Uncle Jee's wheelchair in fury, but Zainab holds her son to restrain him.

Aunty Rabab pulls the wheelchair back. "How dare you?" she gasps. "My husband is a respected member of our community. He has won an award from the President of Pakistan."

Zainab steps in front of Nadia, shielding her daughter from Uncle Jee and Aunty. She glares at them. "Get out," she yells, throwing her words at them like a javelin. "You are dead to me. Get out!"

"You may believe her, Zainab, but no one else will," Aunty says. She smooths out the creases from Uncle's shirt and tightly grasps the handles of the wheelchair. "He would never lay a hand on her. Nadia has him confused with someone else. It has to be. I would be angry at you, Zainab, but I am controlling myself because I know your daughter is dealing with mental issues." She said the last two words softly, as though accusing Nadia of some shameful crime we were trying to keep a secret. She glares at Nadia and continues. "I have always hidden your daughter's flaws in front of the community. But after today, I will no longer do that."

"Get out," Zainab repeats. Her fists are clenched. The veins in her forehead pulsate and her face is flushed. I have never seen Zainab this way. She is always polite and diplomatic, never wanting to cause a scene, always keeping her composure, always wanting to save face in front of others. Today, something has broken inside Zainab—or maybe something has come together. She discards propriety like an overused cloak.

Aunty turns around and pushes the wheelchair down the path to the driveway. The driver helps them into their red Mercedes. Then they drive off, leaving us to deal with the catastrophe that has just unfolded.

27

Upstairs, Jameela is trying to control the havoc that the water from the overflowing bathtub has wreaked. The bathroom is inundated, and the bedroom carpet soaked. She layers towels on the ground and calls frantically for Nisar.

Junaid, Zainab, and Nadia walk slowly through the kitchen into the living room. Nadia slumps into the living room sofa, Zainab covers her daughter with a blanket. Junaid sits in the armchair next to her and holds her hand. His face is flushed.

For an eternity they sit there. Then, Junaid turns on the television to fill the silence. The cricket match is being broadcast, Pakistan versus West Indies. The familiar voice of the commentator is soothing. Zainab and Junaid stare at the television. Nadia's eyes are shut, but she is not sleeping.

Junaid gets up and starts pacing back and forth. "I should've killed him," he mutters.

"Junaid, please. Just sit down."

A few minutes later, he gets up again. "I'm going to get some tea. Nadia, do you want some?"

Nadia shakes her head. Zainab stares at the screen. The batsman is arguing with the umpire.

"Why didn't you ever tell me?" Zainab finally says.

Nadia shakes her head. It is as though she cannot speak.

Pakistan scores a wicket against the West Indies. The crowd in the stadium cheers.

"When you were *seven*?" Zainab asks.

Nadia exhales, "Yes."

Zainab covers her mouth as though to stifle a scream. She scoots over on the sofa and wraps her arms around her daughter.

"I am sorry, I—" Now it is Zainab who can't speak.

The match breaks for advertisements. The biscuit company Peek Freans has launched a new biscuit and their mascot, the Peek Freans Pied Piper, plays his pipe, serenading the children to leave their classrooms and follow him into a land of biscuits.

"When he went away," Nadia says after a few minutes, "I was so grateful. I didn't have to think about it anymore. And I didn't have nightmares. I hoped he had died. And I felt so terrible for wishing that on someone."

Her mother's face is the color of a bleached shirt.

I can see the realization dawn on Zainab all at once. Nadia's strange illness, the doctor not being able to find anything wrong. "This was why you got sick again last year?" she says, slowly. "Because he had come back?"

Nadia rests her head against the headrest of the sofa and closes her eyes.

Zainab apologizes repeatedly, and it seems that with each repetition, the truth and horror of what has happened to her daughter is burned deeper and deeper into her being.

"It was my job to protect you and I failed."

"It's not your fault, Ammi," Nadia says with a sigh. "How could you have known?"

Junaid returns with a teapot and three cups. He sits down on the chair next to his sister and again takes up her hand, gently. There is vitriol in his eyes, but I can see he is trying to tame his emotions, for his sister. "You must drink something warm," he says to Nadia. "You are still shaking. Drink, and then you need to get out of these damp clothes." He pours a cup of tea and hands it to his sister.

Nadia takes the cup. She does not drink it but stares into the cup as if the solace she seeks is to be found in there.

***

Zainab sits with her daughter for hours, holding her until she falls asleep. For the first time in nearly two years, Nadia does not wake with a nightmare. I know it is naive to assume Nadia is going to recover overnight. But I allow myself to hope that the confrontation has taken a weight off her and, perhaps now, she might begin to heal.

Junaid comes into Nadia's room. He insists he will stay the night with his sister, and that Zainab should go to her room and try to sleep. While Nadia sleeps, with Junaid sitting on the chair next to her bed, Zainab stays awake in her room, shrinking under the weight of the day's revelation. She is inconsolable. I feel her spirit being ripped to shreds and I see her outward turmoil and irrevocable guilt at not being able to protect her daughter. She says her prayers and melts to the ground in prostration, staying in that crouched position for the majority of the night. I don't know if she will make it through the night and I worry that grief will take her from us. But when dawn comes, light-footed and hopeful, Zainab gets up from the ground. She showers, changes her clothes, pulls her hair back into a neat bun, and goes to prepare breakfast for her children.

***

Zainab refuses visitors for the next week. They may have meant well, but in these circumstances, it is inevitable that they would come with questions, recommendations, and theories, and she is just done with all of that for a while. She has heard things already from the servants' networks, which have started buzzing. Jameela heard from the driver's brother who worked at Uncle Jee's that Uncle Jee suffered a heart attack that night after he left. He was rushed to the hospital and Aunty had told everyone that Zainab had accused them of terrible things, even after all the support they had shown them over the years, and Uncle Jee's heart couldn't take it. As the day went on, information was exchanged at the fruit seller and the vegetable grocer, exaggerated according to each narrator's whim, and by the time the day drew to a close, the story had morphed into a monstrous version of what had actually happened. Later that day, an enhanced version of the events came back to us like an embellished boomerang, via Jameela's cousin who worked two blocks over.

***

Nadia has begun to leave her bedroom door ajar somedays, rather than closed and locked. It is so surprising and such a pleasure and I notice that sometimes Junaid walks by twice or thrice a day just to make sure it is still open, and I see the relief on his face every time. Some days, Nadia even eats lunch with her mother outside, and they talk and sometimes smile about how when Nadia was little she wouldn't eat rice if it was cooked with cumin, because cumin seeds looked like little insects.

28

1982

Zainab has changed her mind. It is too difficult to stay here, she says. They will move as soon as her waiting period is over. The packers came yesterday to help, but Nadia didn't want anyone in her room. So today Nisar helps her. There is so much to resolve in that room, so much to clean. It is exhausting.

The curtains are open, and the mid-afternoon light comes in through the windowpanes. The books have been packed, and the shoes and sweaters, too. Nisar labels the boxes neatly with a permanent black marker.

"Your handwriting has become so good," Nadia says with a smile. "I'm glad you didn't give up on learning English."

"I tried to quit the tutor every week," he says, laughing. "I made so many excuses. But your mother, God bless her. She didn't give me a choice, forced me, and wouldn't pay me till I studied."

"Ammi said you have a new job, managing a doctor's office. You'll be leaving us?"

Nisar looks sad but excited. "Yes," he says. "But it's not far from here. I will come visit."

"I'm really proud of you."

Nisar puts his hand to his heart and nods respectfully. "Thank you, Baji."

The bookshelves in the room are empty now, as is the desk

and the bedside drawers. The wooden wardrobe lays barren, but Nadia checks the shelves and pulls open the bottom drawer once again, where she used to keep her Magnificent Barbie. Tomorrow is April 24th, 1982, and it will have been four months and ten days since Haji Rahmat passed away.

***

The trucks, two massive eight-wheelers, and one Suzuki arrive early in the morning. They are brightly colored and festive. At another time I would've appreciated them, but today the painted flowers and idyllic landscapes, the perforated metal embellishments, the portrait of Bruce Lee, who has become a local star, seem brazen and unnecessarily celebratory.

The door of the first truck opens, and two movers jump out. One is a slight man in a cream-colored shalwar kameez, the other is broadly built, and his grin reveals betel nut-stained teeth. Neon blue and yellow tassels jingle around the rearview mirror inside the truck. I can't help but feel offended. My family is leaving, and they have arrived in this obscenely decorative truck. Is it too much to ask for a little decorum?

Nadia and Zainab have showered and dressed; both are exhausted from the packing that has consumed them over the past few days. Zainab stayed awake the majority of the previous night; her eyes are dry and swollen from crying, and her expression is that of quiet resignation. Junaid will stay back with Nisar and Jameela to organize the movers and make sure nothing gets left behind or damaged while being loaded.

Nadia asks her brother if she should stay and help with directing the movers.

"No," he says. "Go with Ammi. She needs you. I'll handle this here."

Nadia follows her mother into the silver Toyota.

It is often said that when one nears death, life flashes before their eyes. It must be so because today the past thirty years flash before me in rapid succession. Each room plays a recorded scene, as though reliving its memory one last time before relinquishing it.

In the kitchen, Jameela spreads a dollop of ghee on warm rotis and adds a sprinkle of brown sugar. The comforting scent floats through the house and out the kitchen door. Junaid and Nadia, who have just returned from school, come running into the kitchen with their backpacks and brand-new insulated water bottles.

It is Eid morning and the children are dressed in their new clothes, excited to receive their Eidi. Junaid's kurta matches Haji Rahmat's, Nadia has on a yellow dress of crinkled chiffon and bright pink lipstick which she has acquired in secret from her mother's makeup. Zainab smiles and ladles hot sheer khurma into bowls, and Khansama brings a large tray of freshly fried golden puris to the table.

In the library, Haji Rahmat is enjoying his evening cup of tea; the french doors to the back garden are open. Junaid and Nadia are sprawled on the floor, playing Ludo.

In her bedroom upstairs, Zainab is sitting on her dressing table stool, painting her daughter's nails a rose color to match her own. Nadia blows on her nails to dry them, then jumps off the bed, and turns on the gold musical clock that sits on Zainab's dresser. The gears click into motion and the sound of Beethoven's "Für Elise" fills the room.

It is early morning and downstairs in the living room, Nadia dances in her nightgown as plain tiger butterflies float out of the living room windows.

Today, as the car leaves the driveway, with Nadia and Zainab in the backseat, I feel a crushing, debilitating sense of loss the likes of which I have never felt before.

Nadia turns and looks back at me. Her face is a mixture of sadness and childlike hope. I wonder if she knows that above all, I am sorry, so sorry that I couldn't take care of her.

Now curtains are taken down and folded, and rugs are rolled

up. The fragile items: mirrors, carved consoles, and end tables are protected with bubble wrap. The furniture is wrapped in thick cloth and fastened with rope so it can be loaded easily into the trucks.

The movers start with the bulky furniture items: the beds, the breakfast table, the living room sofas, Haji Rahmat's desk, and armchair from the library. Then they carry the rugs out, which secured tightly with rope resemble dead bodies in bags.

I am empty and exposed.

The movers load the boxes last. Three decades of hope, joy, sorrow, and pain, packed into neatly labeled, corrugated cardboard boxes of assorted sizes are loaded into the trucks.

Thus, I am hollowed out, relieved of my responsibilities. Junaid does a final walk-through with Nisar. They move through the hallways and rooms in silence, two and three times over, to ensure that nothing has been left behind and that none of the windows have been left open. Then Junaid locks the front door and gets into the car. The car reverses down the driveway and exits the front gates, and I am reminded of the words of one of Nadia's favorite poets, T.S. Eliot: *"This is how the world ends, not with a bang but with a whimper."*

29

1983

The dust in Karachi is unrelenting. It creeps in through openings you didn't know existed and settles in nooks and crannies you cannot see, claiming forgotten spaces all for itself.

It is the same with memories. Like dust, they collect, layer upon layer. When you take a broom to a dark corner, wipe down the windowpane, or scrub a marble floor, they reveal themselves and dissipate in the air, bringing to light things you may or may not have wanted to see. Then, like dust, they settle again, laying in wait until the next time you venture into their space, to remind you once again of what was, what could have been, and what may never be again.

It has been almost a year since they left. In the simmering sun of the late afternoon, after a significant amount of cursing and fiddling with the radio knobs, the gatekeeper has settled on an obscure radio station. I hear through the static that there had been a women's protest in Lahore earlier this year. An incensed woman on the radio shares her story, her voice verging on revolution. "There were four hundred of us," she emphasizes. "Not a handful. The government has been downplaying it. The media didn't cover it when it happened in February." The host has a question. "We want our rights of course!" she remarks. "Zia's government is threatened by women wielding pieces of paper! All we want are our rights." The host asks if there was violence at the protest. The woman on the radio is furious now. "Yes, from the police," she says. "There were more police than protestors. They released tear gas into the air and beat us with lathi. I was beaten; many of my sisters were dragged to jail. Shame on the government, shame on the police."

Static fuzzes out the hosts' question but I can hear the woman respond. "History will remember us," she says. "The first and only time anyone stood up in protest to martial law in this country, was a group of unarmed women." When the commentator talks about negotiations, she drowns him out with the words of the poet Habib Jalib. "We can shape our own destiny," she says. "We are no longer going to wait for the writing on the wall that dictates our fates."

The static intensifies and I can no longer hear the rest of the conversation.

I think back to how fearful Haji Rahmat had been when Nadia had joined a protest at her school. He must have anticipated something like this from Zia's government. The gatekeeper shakes his head in disappointment and fiddles with the knobs but the station has been taken off the air.

I wonder how they all are doing. Junaid must be busy with the responsibility of running the business. Perhaps he has told his mother about Rania, that girl whose photo he carried in his wallet. I miss them all. But most of all I worry about Nadia. I just want to know if she is alright.

30

1988

It has been five years since they moved away. Everything is deteriorating. Layers of smut have accumulated on the yellow stone facade, and the marble on the veranda has a permanent film of grime. The interior paint has begun to resemble the dull tan of a drain fly's thorax. Nisar still comes occasionally to keep an eye on the grounds. He has grown a little beard. I didn't think it would suit him, but I must admit, Nisar looks rather dignified this way. The gatekeeper has replaced his radio with a small box television. I appreciate this contact I have with the outside world.

Last month I heard that General Zia-ul-Haq died in a mysterious plane crash. No one knows what happened, but the Pakistan People's Party is being blamed. It hardly seems believable that after so many years he is gone. In a few months, there will be general elections. I don't know if I will be around to witness them. Every day I wait for my inevitable fate—bulldozers coming to level me to the ground, to start the building of apartment buildings on my premises.

But this morning, there is the sound outside of a motor engine coughing to a stop, and a horn signaling for the gate to be opened. The gatekeeper peeks through the peephole. He seems to recognize the car on the other side and goes to retrieve the key that opens the main gate. There is the jangle of keys, and then the grating sound of a key being forced into the padlock before the gates creak open. A car pulls into the driveway, a white Honda Accord. I can't see who is inside.

Nisar steps out first and then opens the back door for someone else.

A young woman steps out. It is Nadia!

My joy and surprise at seeing her again, all these years later, is difficult to express. I have so much to say and so many questions. As always, I can say nothing as she gazes up at me and smiles.

A man I have never seen gets out of the car. He is young and has on a crisp blue shirt and a pair of khaki slacks. His shoes are slightly scuffed, trendy-looking moccasins. He grasps a notepad and pen in his hand, and a Nikon camera is slung on his left shoulder.

"So, this is the place," he says looking up at me.

"Yes," she answers, "this is it. Let's walk around. I want to explain some things to you."

A fiancé? A husband? There is no ring on her finger or his. A prospective buyer? I flatter myself—perhaps he is writing an article about me for a magazine?

"Abbu never wanted us to sell this place, but after he died we had to move away."

"And now?"

"Well, Mr. Ali, now some changes need to be made."

I brace myself. Does she mean changes that involve selling? Is Mr. Ali a real estate agent?

A small bulldozer drives up to the front gate and parks outside. I know now that my end is here, and I resign myself to it with as much grace as I can.

"How does it feel to be back?" Mr. Ali asks.

Nadia inhales deeply, surely taking in the scent of the jasmine flowers before she answers. She is dressed in a printed kurta, lovely in green and beige, and even though the day is warming up, her dupatta is wrapped around her shoulders.

"Bittersweet."

He looks at her in earnest. "If this is hard for you we can leave."

"No," she says. They walk together across the driveway, toward the back of the house. She gazes around at the gardens and the lawn, then the shed.

"Mr. Ali, please have the bulldozer brought back here," she says.

Mr. Ali bites his lip, obviously surprised.

"The bulldozer," she prompts. "They have brought it, haven't they? Bring it here, to the shed."

"Isn't this premature? It would be good for storing supplies."

"Mr. Ali," she says firmly. "Bring them in."

The front gates open and the bulldozer rolls in. It rambles over the driveway, leaving a few crumbled flowerbeds in its wake; squeezes through the pathway between the kitchen door and outdoor washbasins. Nadia waves for it to stop when it reaches the storage shed.

"Right here," she says. "We have no need for this anymore."

The construction worker turns the engine on and drives the bulldozer straight into the storage room. First, the door folds in half like a book snapping shut, and then the concrete and plaster begin to crumble around it in a heap. The bulldozer reverses, and then moves forward, punching its arm and loader scoop into the concrete walls. With the anger of an ancient beast, it barrels through the structure until it is demolished; until the steel beams, the concrete walls, and the tin roof of the storage room all lie in a crumpled heap at its feet. The rumbling reverberates through the ground and within my walls.

"Nadia," Mr. Ali says. "It's rather loud here, would you like to wait inside till it's done?"

"You can wait for me in the front. I am fine here," she says, in a self-assured tone that reminds me of Haji Rahmat.

Two workers collect the remnants of debris in wheelbarrows and wheel it to the front. Now there is nothing left but dust and an outline on the floor where the walls of the storage room had stood.

Nadia kneels and uses her hands to scoop out some damp soil. When she has dug a hole about three inches deep, she reaches into her pocket and pulls out a handful of seeds, which she sprinkles into the cavity. Then she smooths the damp soil over the seeds and pats it down. She brushes the dirt off her hands and her clothes, takes a deep breath, and uses the cuff of her sleeve to wipe her eyes. I notice her fingernails are neatly manicured and painted a pale rose.

Nadia gets up, walks toward the front, and calls to Nisar, who has stayed in the front to discuss some logistics with the gatekeeper. The sun has not yet reached its apex, so the morning still feels refreshing.

I wonder when the rest of the demolition will begin.

Nisar brings the key fob. It jingles, and he tries two keys before the lock of the front door clicks open.

Nadia runs her fingers through her hair repeatedly, nervously, as she waits on the veranda. The dark locks dance in waves between her chin and shoulders. Her face is fuller, and her eyes, green like Zainab's, have regained their brightness from childhood.

She pauses in the foyer, straightens her kurta and her shoulders, and stands with her chin up. The walls bear the outlines of the picture frames that used to hang there. The chandelier that hangs from the ceiling reflects suspended memories. Nadia's eyes are misty. I wonder if she is thinking of what I am, how some twenty-seven years ago, Zainab gave birth to her on the very floor she now stands.

"So, Mr. Ali, the main structure—I want it to remain the same from the outside. This will be the schoolhouse."

I cannot believe it.

She pauses while Mr. Ali takes notes. "The living and drawing rooms—I want them combined with the foyer. How much area is this?" she asks.

Mr. Ali looks around. "I'd guess about fifteen hundred square feet."

"I want this entire space to be an indoor auditorium." She stands firmly and waves her hands in a gesture.

There will be no demolition.

Mr. Ali draws a quick sketch in his notepad.

Nisar unlocks the double glass doors that lead to the family room.

"I'm not sure what to do with this area," she says. "But all the rooms that branch out from here should be classrooms. If we convert the kitchen and guest room, that should be four classrooms on this floor, plus a library. Add the ones on the top floor, and we can have nine classrooms in total." She peeks into rooms as she walks through, and lingers for a few minutes outside her bedroom door.

I am overwhelmed with gratitude and joy.

They go into the library. "The library should stay as is," she says. "It can be expanded later if need be."

They continue into the back garden. Although the grass is dry, the trees are flowering. "Look Nisar," Nadia says. "The jamun tree is bearing fruit."

Nisar tilts his head up towards the tree and smiles. "Would you like me to get you some? Or will you climb the tree yourself?"

Nadia laughs. It is gratifying to hear her laugh. "Actually there is something I'd like you to get for me, Nisar. Remember Ideal Bakery, down the street? Those biscuits used to be so good. Please, would you fetch some? The flower ones with the chocolate buttons, not the jam ones. I want to take some home for Ammi, too."

Nisar heads out to buy biscuits, and Nadia and Mr. Ali walk slowly down the cricket pitch, which is so completely overgrown with wild grass and weeds that it is nonexistent. Mr. Ali takes photos and makes notes. They eventually meander back toward the gatekeeper's quarters in the front. The gatekeeper sets out some folding chairs and a table on the veranda.

"Would you like some tea?" he asks.

"Yes. Thank you," Nadia says, and sits down. Mr. Ali sits across from her and sets his notepad and camera on the table. The sun is almost directly above us now, and the clouds are dissipating. Although there is shade on the veranda where Nadia and Mr. Ali are sitting, soon it will be too hot to be outside.

"So," Nadia says, as though checking off a mental checklist. "I think I've covered the basics. Do you have any questions? Or suggestions?"

Mr. Ali glances over his sketches and notes. "I think I understand. I can always call you if I have questions."

She continues. "I just want this place to be something meaningful, to honor my father's life and the love he had for his home. When we left here, it was soon after my father died, and we were all in a very bad place."

"I can imagine," he says. "It's been vacant for a few years, hasn't it? You must have received many offers to sell, the property has become very valuable."

"Yes, we have. Junaid was ready to sell from the beginning. Eventually, even Ammi wanted to sell, but I couldn't bring myself to sign the papers. Even after everything that happened here, this is still the place I think of when I think of home."

Nisar arrives just as the gatekeeper brings out chai. Nadia is delighted. She opens the brown paper bag and holds it out for Mr. Ali.

"You must have one," she says. "It will change your life."

Mr. Ali grins. "In that case, I shall have two," he says.

Nadia takes a biscuit for herself. It is the same, a chocolate flower dusted with powdered sugar and decorated with a singular chocolate button. She hands Nisar the bag. "Go on, have some. They taste of our childhood."

Nadia swings her gaze around the premises, thoughtful as she drinks her tea.

"When can we begin?" Her voice is earnest. Strong.

"I'll draw up the plans," Mr. Ali says, "and given there are no problems with permits, I think we should be ready to start soon." They chat amicably, sitting on folding plastic chairs on my veranda, drinking tea and eating chocolate biscuits in the midday heat that has chased away the shadows, and I wonder what the future has in store for us.

Epilogue

It has been a few months since Nadia was here. Mr. Ali has come by twice with assistants to take measurements and survey the grounds. Construction will begin any day. The city is abuzz; yesterday we had general elections for the first time in eleven years. An excess of military and police vans have been posted in every neighborhood to handle any skirmishes.

It is the evening of November 16, 1988, and the election results are announced. I can hear the drone of minibuses and rickshaws, the honking of motorcars, and the music blaring from stereos carried through the city on motorbikes. The tricolor flag of the Pakistan People's Party is waving from every rooftop in the neighborhood. Benazir Bhutto has won the general election and is going to be the new prime minister of our country. The gatekeeper has his small television playing, and I see the reporter interviewing PPP supporters, jubilant in their victory. *Benazir, Benazir,* they chant.

"It's a victory on so many levels," the reporter says into the camera. "Since returning from self-imposed exile more than two years ago, Benazir Bhutto, the daughter and political heir of the late Prime Minister Zulfikar Ali Bhutto, has proved, time and again, her ability to draw crowds. And now the thirty-five-year-old Bhutto has reclaimed leadership of Pakistan that many believe was unjustly taken from her father." A montage of pictures flash across the screen: Benazir waving at a victory rally from her motor car while the crowd showers her with rose petals, Benazir dressed in patriotic green and white, her two-month-old toddler in her arm, a garlanded Benazir stepping out of her car, cheered on by onlookers.

I think about Nisar; he must be overjoyed at the Bhutto victory. Haji Rahmat, had he been alive, would have been skeptical as ever. I wonder what change will come with our new prime minister. She is an educated young woman and a new mother. Her victory is unprecedented. My boundary wall is scrawled with 'PPP' in red, black, and green, Benazir's name, and the spear, the emblem of the Pakistan People's Party. I imagine the printing presses working overtime to get the news printed in time for the morning paper. All around me, the night sky is exploding with fireworks and celebratory gunshots. Red, blue, green, and silver fizzle into the sky. The celebrations continue through the night and cease only in the early morning when the muezzin makes the call for prayer. Then the weary stumble home, the dreamers begin to dream, and the city gives us some reprieve before dawn brings with it the hope of a new day.

Acknowledgements

This is a work of fiction, but I am indebted to Yusuf Balagamwala, Farzana Yusuf, Tasleema Adam, Mithi Bai Kassam, Salma Abdul Sattar, Yusuf Sattar, Ruksana Mohammed, Saleh Mohammed, Iqbal Dada, and Peer Mohammed Diwan for sharing their stories with me– I know that my words can never do their stories justice. The following books were indispensable to me as I wrote my novel: *Karachi: Ordered Disorder and the Struggle for the City* by Laurent Gayer, *Dead Reckoning: Memories of the 1971 Bangladesh War* by Sarmila Bose, *Modern South Asia: History, Culture, Political Economy* by Sugata Bose and Ayesha Jalal, and *The Struggle for Pakistan: A Muslim Homeland and Global Politics* by Ayesha Jalal.

Thanks to:

Deborah Reed for her brilliance, kindness, and mentorship.

Chip MacGregor of MacGregor and Luedeke for his advice, and for believing in my work.

Rachel Wickstrom my brilliant editor, and the team at Hidden Shelf Publishing House–Kerstin Stokes, Megan Whitfield and Kristen Carrico–for helping me navigate this uncharted territory with grace and humor.

Gohar Karim Khan, Sanam Maher, Holly Lorincz, and Janel King: for excellent advice, edits and critiques.

My WLA workshop: Sabrina Silver, Stephanie Hortsman, Jeff Amos, Paul Badinka, Jack Wallace, and Rick Krizman. Many years ago, I started some version of this novel surrounded by all of you, and your feedback over the years has been invaluable.

Shanaz Khan, Nurya Shabir, Mariah Haroon, Halima Mohammed, and Afroze Bari, for your enthusiasm.

My siblings, Asma Yusuf, Sophia Balagamwala, and Faraz Balagamwala, for being partners at 12/3.

My parents for making things possible for me. Thank you for buying me books, and for not forcing me to be a doctor or an engineer. It would have turned out to be a sorry situation.

Daddy and Abbujee, for inspiring me, even from so far away.

Zidaan and Deen, for reminding me to laugh.

Ismail, for so much more than I can put into words, and for believing in me always.

About the Author

Sana Balagamwala grew up in Karachi, Pakistan, and lives in Los Angeles, California. She has a BA in English from the University of Southern California and a M.Ed from Loyola Marymount University. She is pursuing an MSt. in Creative Writing from the University of Cambridge. *House Number 12 Block Number 3* is her first novel.

www.ingramcontent.com/pod-product-compliance
Lightning Source LLC
Chambersburg PA
CBHW061208210726
48294CB00006B/1791